He Was Angry.

The set of his jaw and the glitter in his eye told her that. "Stop avoiding me," Dane said without preamble.

"I'm feeding the calf," Tess said hesitantly, indicating the bottle she held to the calf's mouth.

"That isn't what I mean and you know it." He whipped off his Stetson, the quick action unnerving, and knelt beside her, catching her eyes in a lock she couldn't break. "I've tried to tell you that I regret what I did that day."

She flushed. Her heart was pounding. She didn't want to analyze why. "You said so before..." she said, her voice faltering.

"You didn't listen before." He caught her softly rounded chin in his lean fingers and tilted her face up to his. "You must know by now that intimacy can be rough."

"There hasn't been anybody," she said unsteadily. "Not that way..."

Dear Reader:

What makes a Silhouette Desire hero? This is a question I often ask myself—it's part of my job to think about these things!—and I *know* it's something you all think about, too. like my heroes rugged, sexy and sometimes a little infuriating I love the way our heroes are sometimes just a little bit in the dark about love . . . *and* about what makes the heroine "tick." It's all part of their irresistible charm.

This March, I want you all to take a good look at our heroes and—if you want—let me know what you think about them!

Naturally, we have a *Man of the Month* who just can't be beat—Dane Lassiter in Diana Palmer's *The Case of the Mesmerizing Boss.* This story is doubly good because not only is it a *Man of the Month* title, it's also the first book in Diana Palmer's new *series,* called MOST WANTED. As for Lassiter, he's a hero you're not likely to ever forget.

Do you think playboys can be tamed? I certainly do! And you can watch one really get his comeuppance in Linda Turner's delightful *Philly and the Playboy.* Barbara McCauley creates a sexy, mountain man (is there any other kind?) in *Man From Cougar Pass,* and Carole Buck brings us a hero who's a bit more citified—but no less intriguing—in *Knight and Day.* And if a seafaring fellow is the type for you, don't miss Donna Carlisle's *Cast Adrift.*

Some heroes—like some real-life men—are less than perfect, and I have to admit I had a few doubts about Lass Small's *Dominic.* But so many of you wrote in asking for his story that I began to wonder if Dominic shouldn't have equal time to state his case. (You'll remember he gave Tate Lambert such a hard time in *Goldilocks and the Behr.*) Is Dominic a hero? I think he very well might be, but I'm interested in hearing what you all thought about this newly tamed man.

So, I've said all I have to say *except* that I do wish you best wishes for happy reading. Now I'm waiting to hear from you.

Until next month,

Lucia Macro
Senior Editor

DIANA PALMER

THE CASE OF THE
MESMERIZING BOSS

SILHOUETTE *Desire*

Published by Silhouette Books New York

America's Publisher of Contemporary Romance

SILHOUETTE BOOKS
300 East 42nd St., New York, N.Y. 10017

THE CASE OF THE MESMERIZING BOSS

Copyright © 1992 by Diana Palmer

All rights reserved. Except for use in any review,
the reproduction or utilization of this work in
whole or in part in any form by any electronic,
mechanical or other means, now known or
hereafter invented, including xerography,
photocopying and recording, or in any information
storage or retrieval system, is forbidden without
the permission of the publisher, Silhouette Books,
300 E. 42nd St., New York, N.Y. 10017

ISBN: 0-373-05702-4

First Silhouette Books printing March 1992

All the characters in this book have no existence
outside the imagination of the author and have
no relation whatsoever to anyone bearing the same
name or names. They are not even distantly
inspired by any individual known or unknown
to the author, and all incidents are pure invention.

® and ™: Trademarks used with authorization.
Trademarks indicated with ® are registered
in the United States Patent and Trademark Office,
the Canada Trade Mark Office and in
other countries.

Printed in the U.S.A.

Books by Diana Palmer

DIANA PALMER

is a prolific romance writer who got her start as a newspaper reporter. Accustomed to the daily deadlines of a journalist, she has no problem with writer's block. In fact, she averages a new book every two months. Mother of a young son, Diana met and married her husband within one week. "It was just like something from one of my books."

Prologue

***

Richard Dane Lassiter stared down at the city of Houston from his office in the exclusive high-rise building, with eyes that didn't really see the misting rain in the streetlight-dotted darkness. He was wrestling with a problem that wouldn't go away.

Any minute now he was going to have to go into the outer office of his detective agency and chew out his secretary. Actually, she was almost a relative. Tess Meriwether was the daughter of the man his mother had been engaged to. Their respective parents had been killed just days shy of their wedding. So Tess wasn't really related to him, but he'd felt responsible for her for years, anyway. It was why he'd given her this job, why he was so protective of her. There were wounds between them that might never heal, but that didn't in any way diminish his feelings for her.

It could have been love, if he hadn't been so determined to send her running from him. He'd had a failed marriage and he'd been shot to pieces in a gun battle while he was still a Texas Ranger. The shooting had changed him as well as his life. He'd had to give up police work, so he'd founded this detective agency and robbed the local police departments to staff it. He had a reputation for being one of the most thorough and discreet private investigators in the business, and he was very successful. But his personal life was a mess. He had no one, really. No one except Tess, and she backed away whenever he came close. He felt guilty about that sometimes. She didn't know, could never be told, that it hadn't really been anger that had triggered his physical demands on her. She thought he'd been trying to frighten her away. That was funny. The truth was that on that afternoon so long ago, he'd been out of control for the first time in his life.

He turned away from the window, a tall, lithe man with a graceful way of moving and an arrogant tilt to his head. He looked like he'd had a Spanish ancestor from whom he'd inherited his dark eyes, his black hair and the olive tan of his skin. He was a handsome man, but he was unaware of it. These days, he had little use for women.

His own mother had despised him because he reminded her too much of his father, who'd deserted her when Dane was only a child. He'd wanted to love his mother, but she never had time for him. Her attitude had scarred him deeply. He'd married while he was still one of Houston's policemen, before he became a Texas Ranger, but his wife had only been attracted to his uniform. His life with Jane had been a rocky one. She'd wanted something he could not give her. It had taken very little time for her to decide that she'd made a terrible mistake. She didn't want him in bed at all, and very quickly decided that she didn't want him out of it, either. She just didn't want him. When he got wounded, she walked out on him while he was still in the hospital. If it hadn't been for Tess, he wouldn't have had anyone at all throughout that nightmarish time.

Ironic, he thought, that Tess had been in love with him. She'd been only a teenager, just barely out of school, when they first met. Her father, Wyatt Meriwether, had neglected her, just as Nita Lassiter had ignored Dane. Wyatt had left Tess to be raised by her grandmother while he pursued his promiscuous life-style. Tess was innocent and gentle, and she attracted Dane as no other woman ever had. Even now, thinking about how it had been between them during his recuperation could make him ashamed of what he'd inadvertantly done to her.

They'd experienced a tenderness toward each other that was overwhelming in its intensity. He'd fought it at first. He didn't trust or like women, and Tess was altogether too young. But she got under his skin. He'd never been loved like that, before or since. He'd thrown it all away in a moment's passion, and had frightened Tess so badly that she still backed away from him.

He ran an angry hand through his hair. He really had to stop looking back. It did no good.

Now Tess wanted to be an operative. He wouldn't let her. It was dangerous work sometimes. Dane didn't even like sending Nick and Nick's sister, Helen, out on assignments, like the stakeout that Tess had inadvertantly interrupted. He was going to have to give her hell for it. She hadn't blown their cover, but she'd come close. That couldn't be allowed. Besides, he didn't want Tess out in the field. He didn't want her at risk, ever. She kept pestering Helen to teach her things, to show her some martial arts throws, to show her how to use a gun. He usually managed to break up any tutorials, but Tess's persistence disturbed him. He couldn't bear the thought of having her in danger. She was relatively safe in the office, being his secretary. Out of it . . . Well, thank God, he didn't have to worry about that, now.

As for her interference with the stakeout, that was something he *did* have to worry about. He remembered the first time he'd met her, at a restaurant where their parents had invited them to get acquainted. Dane had tried to make her think he'd disliked her on sight. Actually, she'd appealed to him instantly. He almost seemed to know her, which was really disturbing, because he was married and had had his reluctant wife with him that night. Jane had been alternately sarcastic and obnoxious until he'd sent her home in a cab. Tess, on the other hand, had been quiet and shy and very curious about him.

His body began to tauten at the memory. He'd wanted Tess then, and the wanting hadn't stopped during all the years in between. He was resigned to living alone these days. He had a reason for not seeking commitment, for not ever wanting marriage. He couldn't tell Tess what it was. But it was devastating to his masculinity.

With a grimace he started toward the door that separated his office from the waiting room. Putting off the confrontation was cowardly, something he'd never been. It was just that Tess could look so wounded when he scolded her. He hated giving her more pain. Over the years, God knew, he'd given her more than enough.

But she had to learn that rules were meant to be obeyed. If he overlooked this infraction, he might put her at risk in the future. He couldn't have that.

Resignedly, he reached out and opened the door.

One

Tess Meriwether sighed hugely, feeling stiff all over from the tension of waiting for the axe to fall. She glanced ruefully toward Dane's closed office door. Today had really been one of those days. She'd blown a stakeout and gotten the cold shoulder from Dane all day for it. She hoped she could sneak out at quitting time without being seen. Otherwise, she was going to catch it for sure.

Dane Lassiter was her boss—the owner of the Lassiter Detective Agency—but he was also more. She'd known him for years; their parents had almost gotten married. But a tragic accident had killed them both, and the only one Tess had left in the world was Dane.

She carefully put away her equipment with a quick glance at the clock and reached for her trench coat. The coat was her pride and joy, one of those Sam Spade-looking things that she adored. Working for a detective agency was exciting, even if Dane wouldn't let her near a case. Someday, she promised herself, she was going to become an operative, in spite of her overprotective boss.

"Going somewhere?" he asked, suddenly appearing in the doorway, a cigarette smoldering between his lean fingers. He looked like the ultimate private investigator in his three-piece suit.

She had to drag her eyes away. Even after what he'd done to her three years ago, she still found him a delight to her eyes.

"Home," she said. "Do you mind?"

"Immensely." He motioned her into his office. Once she was inside, he half closed the door and came closer to her, noticing involuntarily how she tensed when he was only a few feet away. Her reaction was predictable, and probably he deserved it, but it stung. He spoke much more angrily than he meant to. "I told you not to go near the stakeout."

"I didn't, intentionally," she said, nervously twisting a long strand of pale blond hair around one finger. "I saw Helen and I waved. I thought the stakeout you mentioned was going to be one of those wee-hours-of-the-morning things. I hardly expected two professional detectives to be skulking around a toy store in the middle of the afternoon! I thought Helen was buying her boyfriend's nephew a present." Her gray eyes flashed at him. "After all, you didn't say *what* you were staking out. You just told me to keep out of the way. Houston," she added haughtily, "is a big city. We didn't all used to be Texas Rangers who carry city street plans around in our heads!"

He didn't blink. His dark eyes stared her down through a cloud of smoke firing up from the cigarette in his fingers.

She coughed as the smoke approached her face. Loudly.

He smiled at her. Defiantly.

Neither moved.

A timid knock on the door startled the tall, rangy, dark-haired man and the slender blond woman. Helen Reed peeked around the half-opened door.

"Is it all right if I go home?" she asked Dane. "It's five," she added with a hopeful smile.

"Take your ear with you," he said, referring to a piece of essential listening equipment, "and go with your brother. Nick needs some backup while he stakes out our philandering husband."

"No!" Helen groaned. "No, Dane, not four hours of lewd noises and embarrassing conversation with *Nick!* I *hate* Nick! Anyway, I've got a date with Harold!"

"You were supposed to tell sweetums here—" he nodded toward a glaring Tess "—where and when the stakeout was coming down, so that she wouldn't trip over it."

"I apologized," she wailed.

"Not good enough. You go with Nick, and I'll reconsider your pink slip."

"If you fire me," Helen told him, "I'll go back to work for the department of motor vehicles and you'll never get another automobile tag registration off the record for the rest of your life."

He pursed his lips. "Did I ever mention that I spent two years with the Texas Department of Public Safety before I joined the Texas Rangers?"

Helen sighed. She opened the door the rest of the way and made a huge production of going down on her hose-clad knees, her long black hair dragging the floor as she salaamed, her thin body looking somehow elegant even in the pose. She studied ballet and had all the grace of a dancer.

"Oh, for God's sake, go home," Dane said shortly. "And I hope Harold buys you a pizza loaded with anchovies!"

"Thanks, boss! Actually, I love anchovies!" Helen smiled, waved, and then vanished before he had time to change his mind.

He ran a restless hand through his thick black hair, disrupting a straight lock onto his forehead. "Next the skip tracers will be after paid vacations to the Bahamas."

Tess shook her head. "Jamaica. I asked."

He turned and tossed an ash into the smokeless ashtray on his desk. The entire staff had pitched in to buy it. They'd also pitched in to send him to a stop-smoking seminar. He'd sent them all on stakeouts to porno theaters. Nobody ever suggested another seminar. Dane did install big air filters, though, in every office.

Dane was a renegade. He went his own way regardless of controversy. Tess might disagree with him, but she had to respect him for standing up for what he believed in.

She watched him move, her eyes lingering on his elegant carriage. He was built like a rodeo cowboy, square shoulders and lean hips and long, powerful legs. When he was tired, he limped a little from the wounds he'd sustained three years ago. He looked tired now.

She watched him, remembering how it had all begun. When he'd opened the detective agency, he'd remorselessly pilfered the local police department of its best people, offering them percentages and shares in the business instead of salaries until the agency started paying off. And it had thrived—in record time. Dane had been a Houston police officer years before he made it to the Texas Rangers. He'd been a good policeman. He had plenty of clout in intelligence circles, and that assured his success.

Being a Texas Ranger hadn't hurt his credentials, either, because in order to be considered for the rangers, a man had to have eight years of law enforcement experience with the last two as an officer for the Texas Department of Public Safety. Then the top thirty scorers on the written test had to undergo a grueling oral interview. The five leading candidates to pass this test were placed on a one-year waiting list for an opening on the ninety-four-member force. Dane had been one of the lucky ones. He'd worked out of Houston, ranging over several counties to assist local law enforcement. A ranger might not have to fight Indians or Mexican guerrillas, but since Texas had plenty of ranchland left, a ranger had to be a skilled horseman in case he was called upon to track down modern-day rustlers. Dane was one of the best horsemen Tess had ever seen. Despite his injuries, he still was as at home on the back of a horse as he was on the ground or behind the wheel of a car.

She was awed by him after all the years they'd known each other. But she was very careful these days not to let him know how awed. One taste of his violent ardor had been enough to stifle her desire for him as soon as it had begun.

"You never send me out on assignments." She sighed.

He glanced at her, his expression guarded. He seemed to make a point of never looking too closely, or for too long, as if he found her very existence hard to accept. "You're a secretary, not an operative."

"I could be, if you'd let me," she said quietly. "I can do anything Helen can."

"Including dressing up like a hooker and parading down the main drag?" he mused.

She shifted restlessly, averting her face. "Well, maybe not that."

His dark eyes narrowed. "Or listening to intimate conversations in back-alley motel rooms? Taking photographs of explicit situations? Tracing an accused murderer across two states and apprehending him on a bail-bond forfeiture?"

She let out a long breath. "Okay. I get the point. I guess I couldn't handle that. But I could be a skip tracer, if you'd let me. That's almost as good as going out on cases."

He put out his cigarette angrily, a terse but controlled stab of his long fingers that made Tess uneasy. He was a passionate man, despite his cold control. She very rarely allowed herself to remember how he was with a woman. Just thinking about those strong, deft hands on her body made her go hot and shaky, but not with desire. She remembered the touch of Dane Lassiter's hands with stark fear.

He glanced at her suddenly, his eyes piercing, steady, as if he felt the thought in her mind and reacted to it. She went scarlet.

"Something embarrasses you?" he asked in that slow, lazy drawl that intimidated even ex-policemen.

"I was thinking about having to follow philandering husbands," she hedged. She clutched her purse. "I'd better go."

"Heavy date?" he asked with apparent carelessness.

She'd given up on men some time ago. He wouldn't know that, or know why, so she just shrugged and smiled and left.

The streets were dark and cold. The subdued glow of the streetlights didn't make much difference, either. It was a foggy winter night, stark and unwelcoming. Tess pulled her trench coat closer around her and walked toward her small foreign car without much enthusiasm. Tonight was like any other night. She'd go home to an empty apartment—an efficiency apartment with a tiny kitchen, a bathroom, a combination living room and bedroom, and a sofa that made into a bed. She'd watch old movies on television until she grew sleepy, and then she'd go to bed. The next day would be a repeat of this one. The only difference would be the movie.

Ordinarily, she might go out to a movie with her friend Kit Morris, who worked nearby. But Kit's boss was overseas for two months and Kit had had to go with him—even though she'd groaned about the trip. The older girl was a confidential secretary who got a huge salary for doing whatever the job demanded. Tess missed her. The agency did a lot of work for Kit's boss, hunting down his madcap mother, who spent her life getting into trouble.

With Kit gone, Tess's free time was really lonely. She had no one to talk to. She liked Helen, and they were friends, but she couldn't really talk to Helen about the one big heartache of her life—Dane Lassiter.

She looped her shoulder bag over her arm and stuffed her hands into her pockets. Her life, she thought, was like this miserable night. Cold, empty and solitary.

Two expensively dressed men were standing under a streetlight as she appeared in the doorway of the office building. She stared at them curiously as one passed to the other an open briefcase full of packets of some white substance, and received a big wad of bills in return. She nodded to them and smiled absently, unaware of the shock on their faces as she walked toward the deserted parking lot.

"Did she see?" one asked the other.

"My God, of course she saw! Get her!"

Tess hadn't heard the conversation, but the sound of running feet caught her attention. She turned, conscious of movement, to stand staring blankly at two approaching men. They looked as if they were chasing her. There were angry shouts, freezing her where she stood. She frowned as the gleam of metal in the streetlights caught her attention. Before she realized that it was the reflection of light on a gun barrel, something hot stung her arm and spun her around. Seconds later, a pop rang in her ears and she cried out as she fell to the ground, stunned.

"You killed her!" one man exclaimed. "You fool, now they'll have us for murder instead of dealing coke!"

"Shut up! Let me think! Maybe she's not dead—"

"Let's get out of here! Somebody's bound to have heard the shots!"

"She came out of that building, where the lights are on in that detective agency," the other voice groaned.

"Great place you picked for the drop.... Run! That's a siren!"

Sure enough, it was. A patrol car, alerted by one of the street people, came barreling down the side street where the office was located, its spotlight catching two men bending over a prostrate form in a dark parking lot.

"Oh, God!" one of the men exclaimed. "Run!"

The sound of running feet barely impinged on Tess' fading consciousness. Funny, she couldn't lift her face. The pavement was damp and cold under her cheek. Except for that, she felt numb all over.

"They shot somebody!" a different voice called. "Don' let them get away!"

She heard more pops. Black shoes went past her face, a two policemen went tearing after the well-dressed men.

"Tess!"

She didn't recognize the voice at first. Dane was always so calm and in command of himself that the harsh urgency of his tone didn't sound familiar.

He rolled her gently onto her back. She stared up at him blankly, in shock. Her arm was beginning to feel wet and heavy and hot. She tried to speak and was surprised to find that she couldn't make her tongue work.

He spotted the dark, wet stain on her arm immediately because the bullet had penetrated the cloth of her coat and blood was pulsing under it. "My God!" he ground out. His expression was as hard as a statue's, betraying nothing. Only his eyes, glittery with anger, were alive in that dark slate.

One of the policemen was running back toward them. He paused, his pistol in hand, kneeling beside Tess. "Was she hit?" the policeman asked curtly. "I saw one of them fire—"

"She's hit. Get an ambulance," Dane said, his black eyes meeting the other man's for an instant. "Hurry. She' bleeding badly."

The policeman ran back down the alley.

Dane didn't waste time. He eased Tess's arm out of her coat and grimaced at the gaping tear in her blouse and the vivid flow of blood. He cursed under his breath, whipping out a handkerchief and holding it firmly over the wound, even when she cried out at the pain.

"Be still," he said quietly. "Be still, little one. I'll take care of you. You're going to be all right."

She shivered. Tears ran down her cheeks. It hadn't hurt until he started pressing on it. Now the pain was terrible. She cried helplessly while he wound the handkerchief tightly around the wound and tied it. He shucked his topcoat and covered Tess with it. He took her purse and used it to elevate her feet. Then he turned his attention back to the wound. It was still bleeding copiously, and what Tess could see of it wasn't reassuring. He seemed so capable and controlled that she wasn't inclined to panic. He'd always had that effect on her, at least, when he wasn't making her nervous.

"Am I going to bleed to death?" she asked very calmly.

"No." He glanced over his shoulder as a car approached. He used words she'd never heard him use and abruptly stood as the squad car pulled up. "Help me get her in the car!" he called to the policeman. "She won't make it until an ambulance gets here at the rate she's losing blood."

"I just raised my partner on the walkie-talkie. He's on his way back with one of the perps," the officer said as he helped Dane get Tess into the back seat. "If he isn't here by the time I get the engine going, he's walking back to the station."

"I hear you." Dane cradled Tess's head in his lap. "Let's go."

Just as the officer got in behind the wheel, his partner came into view with a handcuffed man. Dane stiffened.

"M-20's on his way," the officer called to his partner. "I've got a wounded lady in here. Can you manage?"

"You bet! Get her to the hospital!" the other man called back.

The older man wheeled the squad car around with an expertise that Tess might have admired if she'd been less nauseated and hurt.

Minutes later, they pulled up at the municipal hospital emergency room, but Tess didn't know it. She was unconscious....

Daylight was streaming through the window when her eyes opened again. She blinked. She was pleasantly dazed. Her upper arm felt swollen and hot. She looked at it, curious about the thick white bandage it was wrapped in. She stirred, only then aware that she was strapped to a tube.

"Don't pull the IV out," Dane drawled from the chair beside the bed. "Believe me, you won't like having to have it put back in again."

She turned her head toward him. She felt dizzy and disoriented. "It was dark," she mumbled drowsily. "These men came after me and I think one of them shot me."

"You were shot, all right," he said grimly. "They were drug dealers. What happened? Did you get between them and the police, get caught in the crossfire?"

"No," Tess groaned. "I saw them pass the stuff. They must have panicked, but I didn't realize what I'd seen until they were after me."

He stiffened. "You saw it? You witnessed a drug buy?"

She nodded wearily. "I'm afraid so."

He whistled softly. "If they got a good look at you, and recognized the office building..."

"One got away."

"The one who shot you," Dane said flatly. "And they don't have enough on the one they caught to hold him for long. They'll charge him, but he'll probably make bail as soon as he's arraigned, and you're the gal who can send him up for dealing."

"His cohort shot me," she pointed out. "But the one they arrested was there. Can't he be arrested as an accessory?"

"Maybe, maybe not. You don't know how these people think," he said enigmatically, and he looked worried. Really worried.

"I'll bet you do," she murmured sleepily. "All those years, locking people up..."

"I know the criminal mind inside out," he agreed. "But it's different when things hit home." His dark eyes narrowed on her wan face. "It's very different."

She must be half-asleep, she decided, because he actually sounded as if he minded that she'd been shot. That was ridiculous. He resented her, disliked her even if he had felt sorry enough for her to give her a job when her father had died. He was her worst enemy, so why would it matter to him if something happened to her?

Dane stretched wearily, his white shirt pulled taut over a broad chest. "How do you feel this morning?"

She touched the bandage. "Not as bad as I did last night. What did the doctors do to me?"

"Took the bullet out." He pulled it from his shirt pocket and displayed it for her. "A thirty-eight caliber," he explained. "A souvenir. I thought you might like it mounted and framed."

She grimaced. "Suppose we frame and mount the man who shot me instead?"

His black eyebrow jerked up. "I'll pass that thought along to the police," he said dryly.

"Can I go home?"

"When you're a little stronger. You lost a lot of blood and they had to put you under to get the bullet out."

"Helen will be furious when she finds out," she murmured with a smile. "She's the private eye, and I got shot."

"Oh, I'm sure she'll be livid with jealousy," he agreed. I paused beside the bed, his dark eyes narrow and intent her face in its frame of soft, wavy blond hair. He looked her for a long time.

"I'm all right, if it matters," she said sleepily. She clos her eyes. "I don't know why it should. You hate me."

Her voice trailed off as she gave in to the need for rest. I didn't answer her. But his eyes were stormy and his mir had already registered how much it would have mattered her life had seeped out on that cold concrete.

He got up and went to the window, stretching again. I was tired. He hadn't slept since they'd brought her in. A through the operation, he'd paced and waited for news. had been the longest night he'd ever spent.

A soft sound from the bed caught his attention. I shoved his hands into his pockets and stood beside he watching the slow rise and fall of her chest. The unbecor ing hospital gown did nothing for her. She was too thin. I scowled as he looked at her, his mind on the coldness he shown her over the years, the unrelenting hostility that ha eventually, turned a shy, loving girl into a quiet, insecu woman. Tess had wanted to love him, and he'd slapped h down, hard. It hadn't been cruelty so much as a raging d sire that he'd started to satisfy in the only way he knew satisfy it—roughly, savagely. But Tess had been a virgin, a he hadn't known. She'd run from him, in tears, barely time to save her honor. Afterwards, she'd never come ne him again. His pride hadn't allowed him to go after her, explain that tenderness wasn't something he was used showing women. Her frantic departure in tears had sha tered him. She didn't know that.

He'd been antagonistic to hide the hurt the experience b dealt him, so it wasn't surprising that she thought he hat her. He'd even tried to convince himself he didn't mind t fact that Tess avoided him like the plague. To save his pri he'd even made it appear as if his actions had been premeditated, to make her leave him alone.

He thought back to those dark days after he'd been shot. Everyone had deserted him. His mother had always hated him, despite her pretense for the sake of appearances. Even Jane, his wife, had walked out on him and filed for divorce, after being blatantly unfaithful to him. But Tess had been with him every step of the way, making him live, making him fight. Tess had been the light that brought him out of the darkness. And he'd repaid her loving kindness with cruelty. It hurt him to remember that. It hurt him more to realize that she could have died last night.

A faint tap on the door announced the nurse's entrance. She smiled at Dane and proceeded to check Tess's vital signs.

"Lucky, wasn't she?" the woman asked absently, as she waited for the thermometer to register. "Just a few inches to the side and she'd be dead."

The impact of the idle remark was as sharp as a tack. He blinked, his dark gaze steady on Tess's closed eyes. If she died, he'd be alone. He'd have no one.

The enormity of the thought drove him out of the room with a murmured excuse. He walked down the long corridor without seeing it, his mind humming all the way to the black Mercedes he'd had Helen drive to the parking lot for him while Tess was in surgery. He still had to call the office and tell them how she was. He checked his watch; it was time they were at work. He'd stop by on the way to his apartment to shower and change his clothes.

He unlocked the car, but he didn't get in, his hand on the door handle as he stared up at the hospital. Tess wasn't a relative in any sense at all. Their parents had never married. But they were both only children and their parents were dead.

With a rough sigh, he opened the car door and got in. H
didn't start it immediately. He stared at the blood on h
sleeve. Tess's blood. He'd watched it pulse out of her in th
darkness as if it were his own. She could have died in h
arms.

Once she'd been such a bright, happy girl, so eager t
please him, so obviously in love with him. He closed h
eyes. He'd killed that sweet feeling in her. He'd frightene
it right out of her with his clumsy headlong rush at her th
afternoon, when he'd given in finally to the need that ha
been tearing him apart. He'd never wanted anyone so mucl
But he knew nothing of tenderness, and he'd terrified he
It hadn't been deliberate, but maybe, subconsciously, he'
wanted her to back away, before she became his world.
failed marriage made a man gun-shy, Dane thought bi
terly, looking back to the time three years ago when Tess an
he had first met....

From the evening that Tess and Dane had first met—s
long ago, at a restaurant where their parents had invite
them to get acquainted—they saw very little of each oth
except on holidays. Dane and his wife, Jane, were not ge
ting along. And even his mother, Nita, had mentioned ca
tily that Jane had been seen with another man. It was almo
as if it pleased Nita to know that Dane's wife was bein
openly unfaithful to him....

Those days had not been good ones for Dane. Then, c
the morning that Wyatt Meriwether and Nita Lassiter ar
nounced their engagement, Dane had walked into a shoo
out with some bank robbers and had wound up in th
county emergency room fighting for his life.

Tess had rushed to the hospital as soon as she knew. H
father drove her, but when they discovered that Nita was st
at home and that Jane couldn't be found, he'd left.

But Tess stayed, that night and the next day. Once she convinced a floor nurse that he was going to be her stepbrother, and that he had no one else, they allowed her to see him in intensive care. She held his hand, smoothed his brow and cringed at the damage the bullets had done, because she'd had a look at the torn flesh of his shoulder, spine and leg where the bullets had penetrated.

"Will I walk?" he managed in a pain-laced voice when he regained consciousness.

"Of course," Tess said with a gentle smile. She touched his lean face and pushed the hair away from his forehead with a possessive feeling.

His eyes closed and he groaned. "Where's my mother?" he asked harshly. "Where's Jane?"

She hesitated.

His black eyes opened again, fury in them. "She was sleeping with my partner," he said harshly. "He told me...."

She grimaced.

He laughed coldly and went back to sleep.

In the weeks that followed, Dane's life changed. Jane came to see him once, stiffly apologetic, only to inform him that she'd filed for divorce and was remarrying the minute the divorce was final. His mother peered in the door, remarked that he seemed prepared to live after all, and went sailing with Wyatt.

Tess, infuriated with the rest of the family, devoted herself to Dane's recovery.

God knew, he needed someone, she thought. What he'd found out about Jane had very likely distracted him enough to get him shot. Then Jane walked out on him. His own mother had deserted him. Not only that, but he even lost his job, because the surgeons agreed that he might never be fit enough for full-time work again because of the damage to his spine.

When they told him the bad news, he almost gave up, he was so depressed.

"This won't do," Tess said gently, recognizing instinctively the lack of life in his lean face. She knelt beside the chair where he was sitting up for a few minutes and took his hand in hers, holding tightly. "You can't give up, Dane," she told him. "They only said that you *might* not be able to work—not that you *will*. You can't let them do this to you."

"Can't? They already have," he said tersely, averting his eyes. "Why don't you get out, too?"

"You're my almost-big-brother," she said. "I want you to get well."

He glared at her. "I don't need a teenage sister."

"You'll get one, all the same, when our parents marry," she said pleasantly. "Come on, cheer up. You're tough. You were a ranger, after all."

His face closed up. "*Was* is right."

"So you won't be in prime condition for a while. So what? Listen, Dane, there are plenty of things you can do with your law-enforcement background. God doesn't close doors without opening windows. This can be an opportunity, if you'll just look at it in that light."

He didn't speak. But he listened. His dark eyes narrowed as they searched hers. "I don't like women," he began.

"I guess not. With all due respect, your life hasn't been blessed wtih nice ones."

"I married Jane to spite my mother. Not that I didn't want her at the time. She was all set to settle down and have children. That was all she wanted." He averted his face, as if the memory of her desertion was killing him. "Get out, Tess. Go play nurse somewhere else."

"Can't." She shrugged. "Who'll keep you from wallowing in self-pity?"

"Damn you!" he snapped, his eyes flashing warning signals as they met hers.

"Why doesn't your mother come to see you more often?" she asked curiously.

He averted his eyes. "Because she hated my father. I look like him."

"Oh." She moved a little closer, hesitant but determined. "Wouldn't you like to be part of a family?" she asked, sounding more plaintive than she realized. "I've only ever had my grandmother, really, and she only kept me because she had to. My mother died when I was just little. Dad..." She shrugged. "Dad was never much of a family person. So I've really got nobody. And... I'm sorry... but it seems as if now you haven't got anybody, either." She clasped her hands tightly at her waist. "We could be each other's family."

His face had gone hard, and his eyes glittered at her. "I don't want a family," he said deliberately. "Least of all, you!"

"I might grow on you," she said, and smiled to hide the hurt caused by his words. Of course he didn't want her. Nobody ever really had.

He hadn't said anything else. He'd tried ignoring her, but she wouldn't go away. She came every single day, bringing books for him to read, tapes for him to listen to. She cooked for him and sat with him and talked to him, argued with him and encouraged him, and despite his hostility and lack of encouragement, she very quietly fell in love with him.

She didn't realize that her love for him was so obvious. It was impossible not to notice how she felt, when her face was radiant with it. Neither had she known that Dane noticed her without wanting to, his dark eyes growing more covetous by the day as his recovery brought her close and kept her there. He became used to her, enjoyed her, wanted her. She was so different from all the women he'd had in his life. Tess was loving and gentle, and there was an odd kind of vulnerability about her. He thrived on her attentions. He began to look forward to her company.

But even so, he eventually grew uneasy when he began to realize how attached he was becoming to her. He was afraid of involvement, terrified of it, after the disaster of his marriage. Even if he'd married Jane to spite his hard-hearted mother, who didn't approve of her, he'd been attracted to Jane at first, and she'd pretended to be in love with him. Then had come marriage and her distaste of intimacy with him. The crowning touch had been her reckless affair with his old partner on the Houston police force. That had been revenge, he knew, and she'd left him more crippled than the shooting had. Tess was a woman. She could very easily be deceiving him, too, overcome with compassion and what was probably physical infatuation.

His doubts led to a return of his former moodiness, and then to open hostility. He pushed Tess away at every opportunity, but she was stubborn and refused to believe that he really didn't want her around.

He got back on his feet and grew strong much more quickly than anyone thought he would. With good health came a revived male vitality that responded suddenly, and with devastating results, to Tess's femininity....

With her blond hair around her shoulders and wearing a white peasant dress with a colorful belt, she danced into his apartment at lunchtime one day carrying a homemade cake. Dane was in jeans and barefoot, his white T-shirt over his muscular chest damp with sweat from the workout he'd been having in his improvised gym. He limped a little because of his wounds, but he could walk. Now he was intent on walking without the limp, getting fit. But Tess was making him vulnerable all over again, draining him of strength.

He wanted her desperately, even if it was totally against his will. He'd been without a woman for a long time, and he needed someone. Tess was tempting him beyond bearing.

She looked at him with eyes that wanted him, and the need had smoldered so long that it got away from him.

She hadn't seen the calculating look he'd given her as she deposited the cake on the counter in the kitchen, or the warning glitter of his black eyes.

"What's this?" he asked in a sensual tone he'd never used with her before, moving close.

"Just a pound cake," she said breathlessly, her eyes shyly glancing off his as she registered the devastating impact of his nearness on her pulse rate. Her eyes adored him. "I thought you might have a sweet tooth. How do you feel? You look... much better." Her eyes had dropped, as if the sight of him delighted her, embarrassed her.

He hadn't thought about her love life, or lack of it, or it might have prevented what happened next. His only intent at the time had been to ease the ache devouring him, in the quickest possible way.

"I've got a sweet tooth, all right," he'd said softly as he backed her up against the counter and leaned his body into hers. "You must have one, too. You spend half your life devouring me with those sultry eyes. I'd have to be blind not to know what you feel for me. Is this what you want, Tess?" he asked huskily, and moved his hips blatantly against hers, letting her feel the stark evidence of his desire for her. She blushed, but he wasn't looking. His eyes were on her parted lips. "God knows, I want you beyond bearing!"

Her mind had stopped working, shock mingling with fear. Before she could find the words to protest, his hard, hungry mouth covered hers, his hips pushing her against the counter behind her. His hands lifted her into the stark aroused curve of his body, and his tongue went into her mouth with enough lust to make even a virgin aware of his intent.

Tess had only been kissed once or twice, always by men who knew how sheltered her life was. Now she was being subjected to an embrace that only an experienced woman could have responded to, and it scared her to death.

She stiffened and pushed at his chest frantically, but her actions didn't penetrate the haze in his mind. One lean hand possessed her breast roughly while his leg suddenly stabbed between hers in an explicit movement that made her panic.

"Dane . . . no!" she panted, wild-eyed.

He barely heard her. "Yes," he groaned unsteadily. "Oh, God, yes, yes . . .!" His powerful arm contracted. "You want me, don't you, baby?" he'd asked blindly, his body shuddering as his mouth burned over her bare shoulders and throat, only to return, hot and heavy and rough on hers. "Don't you? Right here." He groaned harshly, his hands moving under her skirt, holding her bare thighs as he shifted her so that she could feel the blatant need of his body pressing hungrily at the threshold of her innocence.

She gasped, her heart shaking at the sensations the contact aroused. She moaned under his mouth, frightened.

"Here," he growled. "Right here, baby, standing up," he said shakily. His hands were on bare skin, touching her as no man ever had, as if his own need was paramount, as if she were simply a vessel for that need, to be used.

Then all at once, still breathing harshly, he let her slide to the floor and his head lifted briefly. His eyes were glazed, his body trembling faintly, like the strong, lean hands that smoothed roughly over her breasts as he crushed her mouth under his and groaned harshly. "This is too much for my back," he'd whispered. "We'll have to do it in bed, so that I can lie down. . . ."

She knew it was the only chance she'd have to get away. She ducked and tore out of his arms. Her fear of him was so evident that it managed to penetrate the glaze in his eyes, the raging, headlong helplessness of his need. The threat of intimacy without emotion made her panic. She wept, her sobs loud in the room as she backed away from him, her gray eyes tragic and wide.

"Get away...from me!" she cried as he came toward her, his intentions written in his dark eyes. "Leave me alone!"

It registered, finally, that she was afraid of him. He'd been too drunk on her softness to realize it until he saw the wide, helpless terror in her eyes. He fought to breathe normally. He'd lost control. That was a first.

He stared at her, his expression slowly reverting to its usual impassivity, his eyes startlingly black. "That's what you've been asking for," he said in a cutting, harsh tone as he fought for sanity.

"No!" It was a cry from the heart.

"You wanted me," he spat. "Why else do you keep coming here?"

"I love you," she sobbed, shaken into telling the truth as she stood hugging her arms over her breasts.

"*Love!*" His eyes glared hotly at her as a visible shudder ran through his powerful body, still aroused and hurting. "All right, if you love me, come here. Prove it, you icy little tease," he added with a mocking smile that hid overwhelming frustration.

Her heart went cold, like the tears on her face. She looked at him with anguish. "I can't," she whispered. "You...you hurt me!"

Her fear infuriated him. It was Jane all over again, hating his lovemaking, taunting him, her sarcasm vicious and unforgiving. "No?" he asked coolly. "Then if you won't give out, get out," he added. "All I wanted from you in the first place was sex. My God," he ground out involuntarily as she shrank from him, "why not me? Surely to God you've had others...!"

Her eyes were as big as saucers, her flushed face red, her body shaking. And it dawned on him, too late, that there hadn't been any others. She couldn't look like that, even with him, if she were experienced.

He felt a surge of horror. "Tess, are you a virgin?"

She thought she might faint at the expression in his eyes. She couldn't look at him after that. She grabbed her purse and ran from the apartment. Without a word Dane watched her leave. He didn't go after her; he didn't call later to apologize. It was, he told himself, the only out he was likely to get. Let her think he'd done it deliberately. She made him vulnerable. He had nothing to offer her. It would be a kindness, in a way. He turned back into the apartment, his eyes as cold as he felt inside. He'd never trust a woman again as long as he lived. Not even Tess. A virgin. How could he have not known? He hoped he hadn't left too many scars....

He'd tried to consider it a lucky escape. Eventually, his pretended indifference and hostility had crushed the spontaneity right out of Tess, so that now she was quiet and polite and even a little shy when they were together. After her father died, Dane had offered her a job as a secretary. She had had nobody except him, and he'd wanted to help. It had worked fine, but only when he made her angry did he see any traces of the old Tess. Perhaps, he confessed silently, that was why he kept goading her.

Angrily, he started the car and drove to the office, to be met by the whole staff the minute he walked in the door. It shouldn't have surprised him that his employees loved Tess. She was forever doing things for them.

"Will she be all right?" Helen got in first, her big dark eyes worried.

"She's fine," he assured them. "Still drowsy from the anesthetic, but there won't be any impairment. She has to heal."

"When does she come home?" Helen persisted. "She can stay with me. She'll need looking after."

"She'll stay with me," he said, shocking all of them, including himself. "I'll take her down to the ranch. José and Beryl can take care of her when I have to be in the office. Did you get a temp for the next week or so?" he asked Helen.

"She'll be here any minute," she agreed. "Good typing and dictation speeds and her agency says she's discreet. No worries about loose lips sinking ships."

"Good." His eyes went involuntarily to the desk where Tess worked. It wounded him to see it empty.

"See if you can make any sense out of her appointment book, will you?" he asked irritably, glancing at Helen. "I don't even know what I have on my calendar today."

"You're having lunch with Harvey Barrett," she reminded him. "That's on the extortion case. This afternoon you were supposed to see a couple who want you to find their daughter—the Allisons—and a man who wants his wife watched."

"And this morning?"

She stared at the appointment book and shook her head. "Nothing urgent."

"Good. I'm going to the apartment to change and then I'll be at the hospital until lunch."

Helen frowned. "I thought you said she was okay."

He moved toward the door without answering. "If there's anything important, you can reach me in her room." He gave her the number.

"Okay, boss. Tell her she's missed."

He nodded. His mind wasn't on what was going on around him. It was on Tess.

Two

Tess moaned in her sleep as the pain caught her unawares. She'd been dreaming. Probably about Dane, she thought drowsily. She never dreamed about anyone else. That was almost comical, considering how badly he'd hurt her.

A sound penetrated her semiaware state. She opened her eyes in time to see Dane sitting down in the chair beside the bed.

"What are you doing back?" she asked, her body going rigid. "It's a workday."

"I'm working," he said. "Looking after you."

The wording brought back unbearable memories of the time that *he'd* been shot—and what had followed. She closed her eyes on a wave of pain. "Please go away," she whispered huskily.

He took a slow breath. The anguish in her face made him uneasy. "You don't have anyone else."

That was true. Her grandmother had died a year ago.

Her eyes met his, and there was nothing in her face to betray what she really felt. "You're just my boss, Dane," she said quietly. "That doesn't require you to look after me."

He sat up, his forearms across his knees as he stared at her. "I've never asked. Maybe I need to. How much damage did I do that day?"

She flushed and averted her eyes. "I don't know what you're talking about," she said stiffly.

"Don't you?" he asked on a cold laugh. "We've waltzed around it for three years. I can't get near you, even to apologize."

"Why should you care?" she replied. "You wanted me out of your life. You got it. I wouldn't come near you now for a handful of diamonds!"

"Me or any other man," he said out of the blue.

She pulled the sheet closer, her eyes on the window, not on him. "Don't you have something better to do than bait me?"

"I'm taking you down to the ranch to recuperate."

She went white. She sat up in bed, her eyes like saucers in a face drained of life.

"Oh, my God, don't!" he said harshly. "Don't look like that!"

Her hand trembled on the sheet. "No," she whispered, choking on the word. "Not in your house, with you. Not ever!"

His eyes closed. He couldn't bear the way she looked. He got up jerkily and went to the window, lighting a cigarette as he stared out at nothing at all. He drew in a harsh breath of pungent smoke and let it out.

"I didn't realize you were a virgin," he said curtly. "Not until it was too late and I'd frightened you half to death. Don't you think I know why you don't go out with men?" He turned, pinning her shocked eyes with his. "Don't you think I care about what I've done to you?"

She swallowed, dropping her gaze to her cold, nervous hands on the sheet. "It was a long time ago...."

"It might as well have been yesterday," he said heavily. "God in heaven, stop pushing me away!"

She flushed. "I haven't."

He turned, moving back toward the bed, his face as drawn as her own. He paused beside her. "Tess, I know you're afraid of me physically. I'd have to be blind not to be aware of it. I'm not going to hurt you. I just want you where you'll be taken care of until you're back on your feet again. Beryl will be at the ranch if I'm not."

"I don't know Beryl. Helen says I can stay with her...."

"When Helen isn't at work, she's at ballet class. If she has any free time at all, she's eating pizza with her friend Harold. She means well, but you'd be alone most every evening, and all day while she's at work."

"I'd be all right by myself."

He moved closer, hating the way she stiffened. "Listen," he said through his teeth. "You saw a drug deal go down. You'll have to testify. The policemen didn't actually see the drugs being passed, do you understand? You're the only witness who actually *saw* them. One man is still loose, and he almost certainly knows who you are by now. Do you get the picture?"

"You can't mean what I think you do," she said slowly.

"The hell I can't! I dealt with this kind of vermin for ten years. I know what lengths they'll go to. You aren't going to be safe until they apprehend the second man and bring them both up for trial. I want you where I am, where I can take care of you. When I'm not home, my ranch manager is. He was a ranger back in the forties, and he's almost as good a shot as I am."

She put her face in her hands. It was agonizing to have to agree to what he wanted. She'd almost rather have taken her chances with the drug dealers.

"Hate me, if it helps," he said. "But come with me. Don't throw your life away."

She smoothed back her long, disheveled hair. "What kind of a life do I have?" she asked miserably. "Work and television don't add up to much."

"You're twenty-two," he said. "Years too young to be that cynical."

"Oh, I learned from an expert," she said, lifting her face. "You taught me."

Her expression made him uncomfortable. "I've never had anyone of my own," he said shortly. "My father left when I was a boy. He couldn't take the pressure of responsibility. I worshiped him, but my mother hated him, hated me because I looked like him. Jane said she loved me when we were first married, but she walked out on me and didn't look back." He leaned over her, his eyes black as coals. "You wanted to love me, and I wouldn't let you. I hurt you, made you afraid of me. Don't you get it, little girl? I don't know what love is!"

"You needn't look at me as if I'm any threat," she said defiantly. "I gave up on you years ago."

"Yes. I know."

She averted her eyes. "I don't love you. I had an inconvenient fascination for you that you put into perspective for me. You won't have to fight me off ever again."

His lean hand went to her face. He touched her cheek lightly, catching her chin when she tried to jerk away. His eyes probed hers relentlessly.

"That goes double for me," he said. "I won't ever touch you that way again."

She watched him, too aware of the warm fingers on her softly rounded chin. "You would have forced me," she choked out.

His face contorted. He wanted to deny it, but he couldn't. He'd been out of his mind. "You don't understand," he said bitterly.

She stared at him as if she didn't quite comprehend. He sounded tortured, haunted. "Dane?" she whispered.

He wouldn't look at her. "You were a virgin," he said huskily. "But I wasn't. I'd had women. You were soft and vulnerable and loving, and I wanted you in a way I . . . couldn't handle."

Wheels turned in her mind. Men were vulnerable sometimes; even in her innocence she knew that. She'd avoided the thought for years, but a part of her had realized how desperate he was for her that day, how hungry. "You scared me out of my mind," she laughed nervously. "Every time I went out with a man, I was afraid he might become like that, and I wouldn't be able to get away in time."

"That isn't surprising," he replied. "Will you believe that it hasn't been easy for me, either? You can't imagine what it does to me when you cringe every time I come close to you."

Her chest rose and fell slowly. She searched his eyes. "It was a long time ago, wasn't it? I suppose I blew it up in my mind until it was nightmarish."

He saw the faint softness in her eyes and hesitated. "Tess, is it only fear that you feel when you're with me?" he asked. His eyes fell to her mouth, to the helpless parting of her lips under the intent stare. His thumb moved slowly, the nail just lightly tracing the moist inner surface of her lower lip in a movement that made her breath catch. "Or is there something more, in spite of the way I frightened you?"

She pulled back frantically, oblivious to what he'd said at the last in her desperation to get away from that maddening touch. Her eyes widened and her heartbeat became rushed.

He had to drag his eyes back up to hers. His own breathing was uneasy. So it wasn't all terror. Something inside him thawed a little, even as he watched her futile attempts to hide what he'd aroused in her with that sensuous little brush of his hand. Amazing that in all his thirty-four years, he'd never thought of touching a woman's mouth exactly like that.

"No," he said, almost to himself. "It's a little more complicated than fear, isn't it?"

"Dane..."

"Your doctor says you can leave in the morning. In the meanwhile, there's a uniformed officer outside the door. He's been there since you were brought in, and he'll be there until I take you home."

She watched him nervously as he put out his cigarette.

He caught her scrutiny and his dark eyes slid to meet hers. "You make me want to be gentle. That's a first," he said quietly. He studied her thoughtfully. "Maybe I could make you want my touch, if I tried."

Cold chills worked down her spine. "No," she whispered huskily. "I won't let you touch me. Not the way...you did that day!"

"I've never been with a virgin, little one," he said, his voice deep and slow. "I've never been a gentle man, either, I guess, but I set new records on wildness with you. It made me take a long look at myself. I didn't like what I saw."

Her hands linked together and she looked at them, not at him. "I don't want to talk about it, Dane."

He had to search for the right words. "Haven't you realized by now that most men ... that a man who loved you would want to be gentle? That it wouldn't be like that with someone who loved you?"

"How do you know if someone cares?" she asked with bitter cynicism. She looked up at him. "I thought you did," she said huskily. "I thought you liked me, at least, but you

made me afraid of you so that I wouldn't be a threat to you
privacy. My father didn't want me, either. He landed me
with my grandmother because he didn't want me." She
shivered. "Nobody ever wanted me...." She lay back
against the pillows, looking ten years older than she was
"Please go away, Dane. I'm too tired to fight anymore."

Why hadn't he known how she felt? After all these years,
he still knew next to nothing about her. Of course she'd felt
rejected when her father left her with her grandmother;
more so because of all his affairs. And then he'd planned to
marry Dane's mother, further isolating her. She'd wanted
someone to love, and she'd had the misfortune to pick a
man who didn't even know what it was, who'd known
nothing but resentment and dislike all his life, a man with a
failed marriage behind him and a crippled body to boot.

He grimaced at the defeated expression on her face. He
felt responsible for her anguish, as if he'd caused it. Certainly he'd added to it.

"Do you like horses?" he asked.

"I'm afraid of them."

"Only because you don't know much about them. When
you're up to it, I'll teach you to ride."

Her eyes met his. "Don't do this to me," she said unsteadily. "Please don't. I don't need pity."

He started to speak, but he didn't know what words to
use. He drew in a long breath.

"I'll see you tomorrow. Try to rest."

She nodded. Her eyes closed, blocking him out. She
wasn't going to let him get to her again. No matter what she
had to do to protect herself, he wasn't getting a second shot
at her!

Three

The Lassiter Bar-D was a working cattle ranch. Besides José Dominguez and Hardy, who were horse wrangler and cook, respectively, Dane employed a ranch manager, Beryl's husband Dan, and half a dozen cowhands and other assorted personnel necessary to keep the place running. One man did nothing but look after the purebred bulls. Another took care of the tanks used to water the cattle. Still another was a mechanic.

Tess hadn't really wanted to let Dane spirit her out of the hospital and down to his ranch, but she hadn't been strong enough to fight him. He'd cleared it with the doctor, had had her bags—packed by Helen—already in the car, and the minute she was released, had headed straight down to Branntville.

Tess was uneasy about the prospect of several days in Dane's company. He was acting strangely, and she was nervous—much more so than usual.

He'd never been much of a talker unless he had to social-ize as part of his job, so the trip down to Branntville was undertaken in silence. Tess stared out the window, buried in her own thoughts and occupied with the twinges of pain she was still feeling from the wound in her arm.

"Is that a ranch?" she asked when they reached the out-skirts of Branntville, her eyes on a huge white-fenced prop-erty with a black silhouette of a spur for a logo.

"Yes. Cole Everett and the Big Spur are known all over the state. Cole married his stepsister, Heather Shaw. They have three boys, all teenagers now."

"It's very big, isn't it?" she asked.

"Except for the Brannt Ranch, it's the biggest north of the King Ranch."

"Brannt Ranch? Is Branntville named for the people who live there?"

He nodded and indicated a ranch house far in the dis-tance. "King Brannt owns the spread now. Talk about a hard case," he murmured. "King makes up his own rules as he goes along. He married a beautiful young girl, a model named Shelby Kane, daughter of the movie star Maria Kane. Nobody thought he'd ever marry. He says Shelby came up on his blind side." He smiled mockingly. "He'd do anything for her."

"Did she take to ranch life?" Tess asked curiously.

"Like a duck to water. She and King have a son and a daughter. The daughter, I understand, is sweet on one of the Everett boys."

"What a merger that would be," Tess said.

"They're young yet. And marriage isn't always the end of the rainbow," he added with faint bitterness.

"I guess it has to have common ground, doesn't it?" Tess asked absently, staring out at the horizon. "Two people need more than physical attraction to make a marriage."

He glanced at her. "Such as?"

"Respect," she said. "Shared interests, similar backgrounds—things like that."

"And no sex?"

She shifted uneasily, her eyes on the windshield. "I guess if they wanted kids . . ."

His eyes darkened. "Children aren't always possible."

"I suppose not." She glanced at her hands. "Maybe some people don't mind intimacy."

"Tess," he said heavily. "You don't have a clue, do you?"

She flushed. "Don't I?"

His dark eyes played over her profile, and the fire in his blood kindled. She knew nothing of men and women. It was his fault that she had such hang-ups. He'd hurt and frightened her. Now he wished he'd been different. If he could learn tenderness, it would be sweet to lie with her, to share the beauty of a man and a woman together with her. His body tautened as pictures danced in his mind. Tess, loving him. He could have groaned out loud. He'd thrown away something precious. Ironic that it should have taken a bullet to bring him to his senses, when it was a bullet that had robbed him of them in the first place.

"Here's the ranch."

He turned in between two rows of barbed-wire fences where red-coated cattle grazed. "I share a purebred Santa Gertrudis stud bull with the Big Spur," he explained. "We'll have to replace him pretty soon, though. We've been using him for two years, and that's enough inbreeding."

"I don't understand."

"Are you interested in ranching?" he asked suddenly.

"Well, I don't know much about it," she faltered, her gray eyes darting up to his. "I guess it's complicated, isn't it?"

"Sometimes. But it isn't as difficult a subject as it sounds. You don't ride, either."

"I guess . . . I could learn," she said hesitantly.

He smiled to himself as he rounded a curve, and suddenly they were coming up to a sprawling one-story white wooden frame house with beds of flowers all around it and tall trees.

"How beautiful!" she exclaimed.

Dane's heart swelled at her delight in it. "It belonged to my grandfather," he told her. "He left it to me when he died."

"Oh, it's charming," she said breathlessly. "And the flower beds! I'll bet they're glorious in the spring!"

"They are Beryl's contribution to beautifying the landscape. There are magnolia trees and azaleas and camellias, all sorts of blooming things. She can tell you, if you're interested."

"I love to garden," she confessed. "I've never had anyplace to do it, except in my apartment window, but I used to do all the yard work at my grandmother's house."

He pulled up at the steps and turned off the engine, staring at her quietly. "I don't know you," he said, his voice soft and deep. "I don't know a damned thing about you, Tess."

"Why would you want to?" she asked evasively. "Look, is that Beryl?" A short, white-haired woman had come onto the porch.

"That's Beryl."

"It's about time you got here!" the woman muttered. "Late, as usual. Is this her?" She stopped in front of Tess and looked her over. "Thin and sickly, she is. I'll take care of that with some good home cooking. How's that arm, lovey?" she asked gently. "Still hurt?"

Tess smiled, at home already. "It's much better."

"If you're through running your mouth, I'd like to get the walking wounded into the house," Dane drawled. "She isn't going to get better standing out here in the cold."

"It's not that cold at all," Beryl scoffed. "Why, in little more than a month there'll be flowers everywhere!"

Tess could picture that, but she wouldn't be around to see it, she thought wistfully. She let Dane help her inside, unable to stop herself from stiffening at the feel of his lean arm around her.

"Don't panic," he said curtly as Beryl went ahead to lead the way to the guest room. "I won't hurt you."

She colored involuntarily. "Dane..."

Her reticence made him irritable. "Relax, can't you? You're among friends."

"You were never that," she said stiffly.

"I'm thirty-four years old," he said as they moved down the long hall. "Maybe I'm tired of being alone. You said once that neither of us has anybody else."

"And you said once that you didn't need anyone."

He shrugged. "I've spent fourteen years being a cop. It isn't easy to change perspective."

The mention of his profession made her uneasy. She didn't like thinking about the drug dealers she'd seen or what Dane had said about her being the only witness.

"What's wrong?" he asked.

"I was thinking about the night I got shot," she confessed. "About those men..."

"You're safe here," he said. "Nobody is going to hurt you."

"Of course not," she agreed, and forced a smile.

Beryl settled her in while Dane went out to check on some new cattle that arrived shortly after they did. It was several hours before he reappeared, after Beryl and Tess had gotten acquainted. But the man who walked into the bedroom wasn't the man she thought she knew.

Dane was wearing the garb of a working cowboy. He was in a striped blue western-cut shirt, long-sleeved with pearl snaps, and worn blue jeans under equally worn batwing chaps held up by a wide, silver-buckled belt. He wore black boots with spurs and a battered black Stetson pulled low over one eye. Tess stared curiously. She'd never seen him dressed like that.

"You look like you've been dragged through a brush thicket," Beryl grimaced.

"Not far wrong," he said, nodding. "We had to flush some cows out of the draws. No job for tenderfeet, that's a fact. Are you settling in?" he asked Tess.

She nodded.

He cocked an eyebrow at her. "Well, why the wide-eyed stare?"

"You look...different," she said, searching for a word to describe the change in him.

"I don't have to keep up a businesslike and impeccable image down here," he said with a faint twist of his lips. "This is home."

Her eyes slid away. *Home.* She had an apartment, but she couldn't remember ever having a home where she felt comfortable. Her grandmother's house had been elegant but untouchable. Her memories of the time when her mother was alive were very dim and stark.

"What are we eating?" he asked Beryl, uncomfortably aware of Tess's apparent indifference to him.

"Beef," she replied. "And potatoes. What else is there?" she added with a grin.

"For me, nothing. I'll get cleaned up."

Tess watched him go. Her eyes were more expressive than she realized as she wrapped her arms tightly around herself and almost shivered, remembering the day he'd cured her of hero worship. She'd wanted so desperately to love him, but he wouldn't let her. Now he seemed to want to mend fences. Didn't he realize that it was years too late?

Beryl was giving Tess a curious stare after he left. "You're afraid of him," she said unexpectedly, her expression incredulous. "Honey, he wouldn't hurt a fly!"

Probably not, she thought, but he had hurt her in ways she could never confess to Beryl. "He never liked my father very much," Tess said evasively. "Or me. He's been kind to me since I got shot, but I still feel safer across town from him."

"He isn't like that." The older woman tried again. "Sharp, yes, even hot-tempered, but he isn't vengeful. I've known him all his life. He was a sweet child until his father left. His mother took his father's desertion out on him. I spared him as much as I could, but she was never much of a parent."

"Neither was my father," Tess confessed.

"See, you've got something in common."

"Right. We're both human beings."

Once she got used to the new routine, Tess found the ranch fascinating and the pace relaxing. She insisted on helping Beryl as much as she could. Her arm was sore, but as she told Beryl, the doctor had said it wouldn't hurt to exercise it, to prevent it from becoming stiff. She set the table at mealtime and did what she could to lessen the strain of her presence, and she enjoyed the warmth of the other people who lived on the ranch.

But she carefully kept her distance from Dane, to his dismay. There was always some reason why she had to leave a room once he entered it, why she had to be unavailable if he was in the living room after dinner, instead of in his study working.

In the office, their relationship was strictly professional. She took dictation, answered the phone and kept things running smoothly. But here, where he was in his element, he was a different man. She had trouble adjusting to him on a personal level. Even when he'd been shot, he'd been the professional lawman, except for that once. And it had happened at the apartment he kept in town, not here at the ranch. If he had an inner sanctum, this was it. This was the first time she'd seen it; he'd made sure of that.

Here, away from the world, he was relaxed and not so severely on his guard. He limped a little because of the primarily physical work he did on the ranch, and his temper was more noticeable than at the office, but he was also less driven and stoic. That fact was what made Tess so nervous. She was vulnerable here, away from prying eyes. Beryl never intruded. Neither did any of the ranch hands. It made her uneasy to be totally at Dane's mercy.

He noticed that she avoided him and became impatient with it. And finally, three days later, he confronted her while she was helping feed a stray calf in the barn.

He was angry. The set of his jaw and the glitter in his eyes would have told her, even without the taut stance of his body.

"Stop avoiding me," he said without preamble, his very tone intimidating.

She looked up at him nervously. She was wearing jeans and a denim coat over her blue blouse, with her hair plaited at her nape. She looked very pretty, even without makeup, something Dane noticed.

"I'm feeding the calf...." she said hesitantly, indicating the bottle she was holding to the calf's mouth as she balanced its small head on her knee.

"That isn't what I mean, and you know it." He whipped off his Stetson, the quick action unnerving, and knelt beside her. He was in working garb, too. His jeans and boots were much more disreputable-looking than hers, his batwing chaps stained and worn. The cuffs of his long-sleeved chambray shirt were speckled with mud and blood, like the sleeves of his open shepherd's coat. He looked up, catching her eyes in a look she couldn't break. "I've tried to tell you that I regret what I did that day," he said roughly.

She flushed. Her heart was beating her to death. She didn't want to analyze why.

"I thought you were more experienced than you turned out to be, or I wouldn't have taken it that far, that fast."

"You said so before," she faltered.

"You didn't listen before." He ran his hand through his thick, damp hair. "You go out with men occasionally. You must know by now, at your age, that intimacy can be rough."

She looked down at the calf. She didn't answer him.

"Right?" He caught her softly rounded chin in his lean fingers and tilted her face up to his. "Tell me."

"There hasn't been ... anybody," she said unsteadily. "Not ... that way."

His face changed all at once. He frowned slightly, his eyes falling to her parted lips and then back up to her eyes. "How deep are the scars I gave you?" he asked quietly.

Her thin shoulders moved restlessly. "Pretty deep," she said with a humorless laugh. "Dane, I have to finish this."

He withdrew his hand, draping it across his knee as he watched her. Her reaction to him was damning. He made her nervous. He could see her hands shaking, and he hated that part of the past that was responsible for her helpless fear.

"You kept coming, no matter how hard I tried to push you away. You got closer than anyone else ever had," he said without meeting her eyes, his fingers tracing a streak of mud on the knee of his jeans as the involuntary confession escaped him. "I got in over my head before I knew it. I didn't really want a woman in my life."

"But you were married once, before you got shot," she said.

His eyes met hers and he smiled with pure mockery. "I started dating Jane because my mother didn't like her. Then I married her because she wouldn't sleep with me any other way. But she only suffered me in bed for one reason," he said, without elaborating on the reason. His face hardened. "Eventually she went looking for a man who could give her everything she needed. I assume she found him when we were divorced. She's remarried and has a child."

"Oh." She frowned, her eyes searching his curiously as she tried to get up enough courage to ask a question that was gnawing at her.

"You want to know why she didn't like sleeping with me," he said, nodding. "Do you really need to ask?"

He was like a bulldozer, in every way. Perhaps the ardor he'd shown her that long-ago day was how he made love naturally. She hadn't considered that likelihood.

It opened her mind to new possibilities. She lifted her face. "Was it...were you that way with her? Like you were with me that day?"

His jaw tautened. "I've never liked a woman enough to care whether or not she enjoyed me in bed," he said bluntly. "I wanted Jane. I thought if she loved me, preliminaries wouldn't matter."

Her breath escaped in a sigh. She was innocent on certain subjects, but she seemed to know more about than he did.

"But...but you can't just...just..." She colored. "Dane, women aren't like men," she said helplessly. "A woman has to have time, tenderness."

"How would you know?" he asked insolently. "Didn't you just practically admit to me that you're still a virgin?"

The blush got worse. She glared at him. "Being innocent doesn't make me stupid. I watch movies and read books, you know. I do have some idea of what a woman is supposed to feel with a man she loves."

"You loved me," he said darkly. "And you felt nothing except fear."

"I was infatuated with you," she corrected, shivering inside at the knowledge that she'd been so transparent. At nineteen, she'd known nothing about how to keep her heart hidden. "You hurt me, and not just emotionally."

"That wasn't deliberate. I was...hungry for you," he said hesitantly. He sounded almost vulnerable. "You were sweet and loving, and I thought..." He cursed under his breath. "What does it matter?" His eyes darted up and slammed into hers. "You didn't want me."

"You were so violent," she whispered weakly.

His fist clenched on his knee. "I don't know any other way with a woman!" he said stiffly. His eyes narrowed as they met hers. "I was a late bloomer. My mother was the only woman I'd been around much and she hated men with a vengeance. In fact, she hated me, too. I got my first taste of women when I was a rookie cop. The kind of women you meet out on the streets in police work are every bit as tough as the men, because they have to be. The only encounters I ever had were rushed and unemotional." His eyes were unconsciously intent on her face. "The way I was with you that day...is the only way I know."

"Dane," she whispered, her voice soft with unwilling compassion. "I'm so sorry!"

His dark eyes met hers. "What?" he asked absently.

She wondered if he realized what he'd told her, how much of himself he'd revealed. She reached up, for the first time voluntarily touching his lean cheek. Her fingers were cold.

He jerked back from her, his eyes glittery, and closed up like a clam. "I don't need pity, honey," he said mockingly. "I don't need a damned woman, either."

He got up and stomped off down the aisle, leaving a shocked, puzzled Tess behind.

* * *

For the next two days, it was Dane who avoided her, almost as if his confession had embarrassed him. Tess found herself less nervous as she considered how his attitude toward women had stifled his ability to feel tenderness.

Tess had never really liked his mother—Nita Lassiter had been very brittle, very flighty. When Tess's father wasn't around, she was all but hostile toward Tess, and even more so toward Dane.

Dane's ex-wife hadn't seemed much of a prize, either, judging from that one dinner Tess had spent with Dane and her. Her sullen, resentful behavior had convinced Tess that the woman had never loved Dane, and he himself had said that it was the uniform that had attracted Jane more than the man inside it. Jane had struck Tess as being just as much a man-hater as Dane's mother.

She frowned thoughtfully. Didn't they say a man unconsciously looked for women who reminded him of his mother? Or that men sometimes, equally unconsciously, chose women who lived down to their image of them? Dane had spent his time around women of questionable character in his youth, so perhaps he thought sex was only permissible with women who had no softness, no vulnerability.

It was a sobering thought. But she had no time to work on the theory, because Dane announced suddenly that he'd been away from the office long enough and had to get back. Naturally, Tess agreed to return to work, too, because her arm was back to normal, even if a little soreness remained.

He packed and drove them back to Houston, silent and unapproachable, after Tess had said her goodbyes to Beryl.

"I'm going to post a man outside your apartment, and I'm having you followed," he said curtly when he deposited her suitcases in her apartment an hour later.

She looked up at him irritably. "I don't need a watchdog. I'm perfectly capable of calling the police if I need to."

"No, you aren't," he replied. "You don't know these people. I do."

"Mr. Policeman." She nodded, eyes flashing at him. "I'll bet when you were a beat cop, your badge was sewn to your skin!"

He smiled, a sensual twist of his lips that made her heart race. "I loved the job," he agreed. "It was, and is, the only place I feel comfortable, apart from the ranch. Detective work isn't so different from what I did. Especially when I take a criminal case."

That was a fact. During the time she'd worked for him, she'd known him to track down murderers and bank robbers, to subdue them and bring them in, all as part of the job. Returning fugitives for worried bail bondsmen was a big chunk of the agency's income. Tame cases he left to the skip tracers and operatives. He took the dangerous ones—he and Nick, his protegé.

"It's the adrenaline," she murmured. "You're addicted to the danger."

"Am I?"

"It would explain why you won't slow down," she said. Her eyes slid down the muscular length of him, over the scarred shoulder and chest she knew were hidden under his clothes.

"You wouldn't want to look at me after the damage the bullets did," he said quietly. "It would make you sick."

Her eyes jumped back to his. "I was thinking about how it happened," she said. "Not how it would look."

He relaxed a little, but not much. He always seemed as if his spine were glued to a wall. He walked tall, never slumped or slouched. His posture, like his character, was arrow-straight.

"All the same, I'll never be anyone's idea of a pinup in a bathing suit," he said with a faint smile. "Not that I was before I got shot."

Her unblinking stare was involuntary. "I've never seen you in a bathing suit," she remarked absently.

He didn't move, but his eyes darkened, became intent on hers. "I wouldn't be caught dead in one, now. Not in public, anyway." His chest rose and fell heavily. "I'd let you look at me, I guess. But no one else."

Her body stilled as she looked up at him. "Why me?" she asked softly.

"Because you wouldn't make me feel like less of a man," he said simply. "Some women have a knack for putting a knife in a man's ego. It makes them feel superior. When a man does the same thing to a woman, they call him a chauvinist. Some double standard."

"All women aren't like that."

He moved a step closer to her. When she didn't tense or move back, he took another step, and another, until he was close enough to smell the faint scent of violets that clung to her skin. She was wearing a soft gray pantsuit with a heather-colored jacket. Her hair was loose and she looked young and pretty and very vulnerable.

He caught a handful of her hair a little roughly and pushed up at her nape to lift her face to his narrow, darkening eyes.

"Teach me," he said huskily.

Her lips parted on a rush of breath as her heartbeat ran wild. "Wh-what?" she whispered.

His eyes fell to her mouth and he bent toward it, his own mouth parting just as it touched hers. "Teach me how to be gentle...."

He spoke the words into her mouth. She stiffened at the moist, hot pressure, the smokey warmth of his own mouth so intimately touching hers. She could breathe him, smell the tang of cologne, feel the strength and power of his body almost touching her.

His eyes were open, and she looked into them just as his lips brushed hers.

"What do you like, Tess?" he whispered. His teeth opened and closed with exquisite tenderness on her upper lip, while his tongue softly tasted its moist inside. "Tell me."

Her hands were on his chest, under the tweed jacket, against his white shirt. Under the material, she could feel a thick cushion of hair over hard, warm muscle. "Dane, you can't," she began shakily.

"Why?"

His mouth was easing her lips apart. The contact was making her knees weak. "You hated...me," she whispered.

"I hated my mother," he corrected, his eyes searching hers while he played with her mouth, that steely hand at her nape still clutching her soft hair, "I hated my ex-wife...I hated half the world. But I never hated you." His heavy brows drew together in something like pain. "Never, Tess...!"

She felt him shudder as his mouth came down completely over hers, capturing it in a silence that danced with tension, with impossible desires.

For an instant, it was like the past again. But his arms weren't bruising. She could feel the restraint in him, the determination to go slow, to not rush her. Because of it, and because of what she'd learned about him, the panic began to recede. She let him hold her. And for the first time, she allowed herself to feel his mouth, to let herself taste it as he kissed her with exquisite softness. The contact was more pleasurable than she'd ever dreamed. His lips were firm, and he tasted of coffee. She liked the way he tasted.

As the pleasure grew, she felt a sudden heat in her lower body, a faint trembling in her legs. "Dane..." She heard her voice sobbing against the pleasure of his mouth, but like lightning striking, his hand contracted and he ground her lips apart under his, so that his tongue could ease between her teeth and push softly inside the sweet darkness of her mouth.

She remembered the one time she'd shared a deep kiss with him and gasped.

He lifted his head slowly, his heart pounding with a heavy beat. He looked down into her shaken eyes for a long moment, fiercely satisfied with what he saw there. She wasn't afraid; she was aroused. Amazing, that tenderness could make such a difference. It enhanced his own pleasure.

But he read the hesitation she couldn't disguise. "You don't like deep kisses with me, do you?" he asked huskily, his eyes glittering with desire. "My tongue pushes inside your mouth, penetrates it, and you shiver because of the images it produces." His hand loosened on her hair, smoothing it. She stood quietly against him, not protesting, as his deep, soft voice held her captive. "It's very much like another kind of penetration," he breathed, nibbling at her mouth. "Intimate, and urgent, and very, very deep...." He whispered into her mouth, suiting the action to the words as his tongue probed slowly.

She cried out and suddenly lifted her arms convulsively around his neck, at almost the same moment that the telephone jangled noisily in the heated silence.

Her body jumped, and her wounded arm throbbed, even as his head lifted with a faint groan. Her eyes were wild, frightened all over again. She was trembling, but this time not because of fear. She was clinging to him, not fighting him. He'd aroused her. The knowledge made his heart slam at his ribs.

She couldn't stand. Her knees gave way when he let go of her.

"It's all right," he whispered, lifting her in his arms. "I've got you."

She laid her cheek against his jacket, clinging to him weakly as he carried her to the sofa and sat down with her in his lap before he answered the telephone.

"Yes, she's back. Yes, she's all right. No, you can't speak to her. I'll have her call you later," he said tersely.

He hung up. "Helen," he murmured dryly, looking down into her dazed eyes. "Checking to see if you were home."

"That was nice of her."

"Yes, it was, but her timing stinks," he said huskily. His eyes fell to her mouth. "I'm glad that I can make you want me, Tess."

"That's conceit..." she began.

His mouth covered hers, parting her mouth, making her cling to his strong neck. He didn't increase the pressure or deepen the kiss. He stroked her mouth with his for a few aching seconds and then lifted his head. He looked at her with pure hunger until she flushed and averted her gaze to his throat.

"I've never kissed anyone like this," he whispered after a minute.

"Neither have I." Her cheeks flushed with heat. "The things you said to me...!"

"Turned you on so much that you gasped," he murmured, his eyes glittering. "I've never said things like that to another woman. They seem to come naturally with you."

"You didn't hurt me."

His jaw tautened. He looked at her mouth until his body began to ache. He was getting in over his head here. He had to stop, now, while he still could. "No," he returned deeply. "I didn't hurt you." He'd never tried to be gentle. Tess made him want that. Made him want things he resented wanting. "I couldn't hurt you now. Not even if I wanted to."

He nuzzled his cheek against hers with rough affection and hugged her close for an instant before he made himself put her gently away and get to his feet. "I'd better go. Keep the door locked. Get some rest. We'll try to restore order to the office in the morning, if you're sure you feel up to a day's work."

"Of course I do," she stammered. Her hair was disheveled, and her mouth tingled. She stared at him helplessly as he straightened his tie. "Why?" she whispered.

He was still getting himself back together. He'd never felt such a weakness for a woman, such a raging need to please, to pleasure her. He hadn't thought he was still vulnerable, but he was. He wanted Tess as he'd never wanted another woman. He couldn't afford to give in to it. Not now. Not yet.

His dark eyes pinned hers. "Remuneration for past sins?" he asked, lifting an eyebrow as he smiled mockingly.

Her face fell. "Oh."

Her naked vulnerability took the sting out of his hunger for her. He took a long breath. "Hell!" He laughed harshly. "I'm a loner, have you forgotten? None of this is easy for me." He pulled a cigarette out of his pocket and lit it with a flick of his lighter. "I wanted to know that I could arouse you, that I could make you stop being afraid of me, all right?" he asked irritably.

"Only that?"

"No. You know, you must know, that I want you so much I can hardly bear it." His eyes dropped to her mouth. "Don't let me get that close again, for your own sake," he said finally, turning away. "There's no future in it. Let's just say that I wanted to see if tenderness had any selling points."

"Does it?"

At the doorway he turned, the knob already in his hand. He didn't answer the question. He looked at her with quiet desperation. "Tess, I'm set in my ways, too jaded and hard for a little puritan like you. I'll probably always want you, but I don't want commitment. That being the case, you can't let me seduce you. Let's keep some distance between us, okay?''

She forced a smile. At least he was honest. And some of those old scars were smoothing out, because of what had just happened. "Okay. Thanks for taking care of me, when I needed help."

"I'll always be around if you need me, baby," he said gently.

The casual endearment made her pulse race. She couldn't hide her reaction to it from him.

"You remember the last time I called you that, don't you?" he asked quietly. "Despite the way I just was with you, in bed I'm rough and quick and my pleasure comes first," he said with brutal honesty. "Virgins aren't my style, and I'm sure as hell not yours." He drew in a slow, regretful breath and his lips twisted. "So let's quit while we're ahead. Good night, Tess."

He went out and closed the door. She went to it, her fingers touching the doorknob with exquisite care, as if she could still feel the warmth of his hand there. He'd just walked out on her for the second time, except that now she wasn't afraid of him anymore. She was back in her old rut, teetering on the knife-edge of love, with no way to go but down.

Four

Dane hadn't relented on the subject of Tess's bodyguard. One of the operatives, a free-lancer named Adams, was two steps behind her all the way to work.

Helen grinned when she came into the office. She sang a few lines from "Me and My Shadow" and did an impromptu tap dance.

"Oh, shut up," Tess grumbled. "Dane thinks I'll be killed in broad daylight, I guess."

"He can't take the chance," Helen whispered, wiggling her eyebrows. "Think of the damage it would do to the agency's reputation if our own secretary bit the dust with us guarding her!"

Tess burst out laughing. "You raving lunatic." She hugged the other girl warmly. "It's good to be back to work."

"We missed you," Helen asserted. "Nobody hid under my desk all week."

"I don't hide under your desk."

"You would have, but there isn't room, what with my feet and the trash can I keep under there. I'm really sorry I forgot to tell you about that stakeout," she said with a grimace. "Dane in a temper is a sight to behold, isn't he?" She sighed. "Although sometimes I think it's too bad I'm committed to Harold. I could go for Dane in a big way." She frowned thoughtfully. "He hasn't dated anyone since his ex-wife left him, has he? Do you think it's because he got shot?"

"What do you mean?" Tess asked curiously.

"I mean, he limps sometimes," the other girl replied, careful to make sure they weren't being overheard. "It might cramp his style in bed."

Tess cleared her throat. "It doesn't cramp it on a horse," she said. "He was out helping round up new calves while I recuperated at the ranch."

"Good point." Helen shrugged. "Maybe he thinks he's unsightly. Or maybe he just hates women. What a waste of a good man. If only he didn't have that textbook police officer's face. He hardly ever smiles, and everything is always business with him." She shook her heard and turned away. "I wonder if he's like that with a woman."

Thinking about how Dane was with a woman made Tess's knees go weak. The things he'd whispered to her when he kissed her weren't dry as dust, for a fact. He might be rough, but he was sensual, and she was just discovering—as he seemed to be, too—that he could be very tender....

"Catch me up, will you?" Tess asked as she uncovered her computer. "I feel as if I've been away for a month."

"I don't doubt it. Arm okay?"

"A little stiff." She grinned at Helen. "No need to worry. We tough, dedicated professionals can take the odd gunshot in our stride."

"Rub it in," Helen groaned. "Now, everybody in the *office* has been shot except me. Even the secretary!" she added with a hot glare at Tess.

Tess raised her hands. "Not my fault. I swear I didn't invite those men to point a gun at me, not even to get one up on you."

"Oh, yeah?" Helen propped her hand on her hip. "How do I know that?"

The office door opened and Dane glared at them. "On company time, you work. Get busy."

"Yes, sir," Helen said demurely.

Tess couldn't quite meet his eyes. She sat down at her desk. "Helen was going to catch me up."

"Make sure it's business, not play," he said tersely.

She glanced at him. "You look tired."

"I didn't sleep." He ran a hand through his dark hair, letting his eyes dart off hers without lingering. "When Andrews calls, have him drop by the office about lunchtime. I've got an assignment for him. I'll be in conference with the skip tracers. Hold my calls until I'm through."

"Will do."

His dark eyes slid over her face and down to the rounded neckline of the red blouse that went with her cream-colored suit. Her hair was in a chignon and she was wearing only a trace of makeup. "You look very elegant this morning," he said unexpectedly. "Lunch date?"

"No." She fiddled with the keyboard. "I didn't want to disappoint my shadow by dressing like a boring office girl. I thought he might be more impressed if I put on my Mata Hari outfit."

He cocked an eyebrow. "Wrong genre. We're detectives, not spies."

"It wouldn't be the same if I wore a trench coat and an Indiana Jones hat."

"Maybe not." He stuck his hands in his pockets. There was something preoccupied in his manner.

She hadn't missed the black scowl. "What's wrong?"

He let out a hard sigh. "Your assailant jumped bail. He's out on the streets and nobody knows where."

Her arms felt chilled. She didn't have to ask why that worried him. It was disturbing and frightening to know that she was the only witness to a drug deal. What she'd seen could send two men to prison. If they were desperate enough to silence her, her life wouldn't be worth a plug nickel.

"Adams had me in sight constantly this morning," she said.

He nodded. "He's one of the best. But having you in sight won't be enough. He can't sleep with you."

"You could teach me how to use a pistol."

"It takes years of experience to shoot one properly," he reminded her. "And it isn't the same when you're in a desperate situation, as when you're on the practice range."

He would know, she thought, watching him. He'd been in enough desperate situations over the years. "I could move in with Helen," she suggested, as she had once before.

He took his hands out of his pockets and sat on the edge of her desk, leaning forward so that none of the others in the office could hear him. He stared at her intently. "Don't take this the wrong way. I'm not making improper suggestions. But I want you to move into my apartment until we catch your assailant."

"Live with you?" she asked hesitantly.

He nodded. "It's the safest way. I'd let you move in with Adams, but his girlfriend wouldn't like it," he murmured dryly, trying to lighten the moment.

She hesitated.

"Tess," he said quietly, "if you're worried because of what happened last night, there's no need. I told you that I don't want commitment. I won't seduce you. And you must know by now that I won't force you, either."

She bit her lower lip. "Yes, but it wouldn't look right."

"No one will know except the office staff," he promised her. "And they know why. It isn't as if I'm asking you to have an illicit affair with me."

"I know that." She stared at her pink fingernails. The thumbnail was chipped. She picked at it nervously.

He tilted her chin up and smiled faintly. "I won't walk around in the nude or watch football games for the duration."

She smiled in spite of her fears. "Do you normally watch football games?"

He shook his head. "But I do normally walk around nude. I'll have to buy a pair of pajamas while you're in residence. And a robe."

"I like pajamas, too," she said.

"I'll pick you up tonight at seven and take you home with me," he said. "Until then, Adams can keep an eye on you."

He got up from the desk. Tess felt more uncertain than she ever had before. Living with him was going to be one big test of her immunity to his attraction.

With a frown she watched him go back into his office. Why was he doing it? To prove to himself that he really didn't want her? She wished she knew. But she was much too afraid of the consequences of staying by herself to argue with him. Over the years she'd learned how cheap life was to people who used and sold narcotics. Dane was a trained policeman, an ex-Texas Ranger who knew more about means and methods of protecting people than she had time to learn. She was glad he had that knowledge. Now, her very life might depend on it.

The day turned out to be a quiet one, thank goodness. She left at five with Adams on her heels, and when she got home, packed enough for a few days. She didn't like leaving her apartment, but she really had no choice.

Dane buzzed the apartment at seven sharp, and she opened the door.

"Ready?" he asked.

"I've just got to get my coat," she said, looking around. She had a single suitcase.

"Is that all you're bringing?" he asked with a frown.

"Well, it's enough for a few days," she began.

"Tess, this could take weeks," he said shortly. "I don't want to alarm you, but you may be with me for some time."

"I—I can come back and get what I need, can't I?"

"I suppose. Did you pack a gown and a robe?"

"Yes." She flushed. "Well, pajamas and a robe."

He smiled gently. "You'll have your own room. It's a big apartment."

"I remember," she said absently, and then regretted dragging the memory up when he glowered.

"Let's go," he said tersely.

She locked up. He carried her case down to the garage, his eyes watchful and alert to any sign of danger. She noticed with quiet resignation the faint bulge under his jacket. He carried a .45 automatic pistol on the job. He had a permit for it, and it was registered. A tool of the trade, he called it. But to Tess, it was a painful reminder of the ever-present danger of his profession and the realization that he could be killed pursuing it.

He helped her into the car before he put the case in the trunk, and he examined the engine and every inch of the frame before he started the vehicle.

"Is that necessary?" she asked.

He nodded as he backed out of the parking space. "Part of the routine, honey. Don't worry about it. You're in good hands."

"I know that." She leaned back against the seat. "Why did I have to leave the office late?" she groaned. "If I'd gone home when I should have that night, I wouldn't have seen anything."

"I was busy calling you on the carpet," he reminded her with a glance. "I get to share the blame."

"I deserved it, blowing the stakeout that way."

"In fact, you saved it," he murmured reluctantly. "The storekeeper had grown suspicious of our people outside. When you waved to Helen and asked about Harold's nephew, he grew careless. They collared his son five minutes after you left."

Her jaw dropped. "You didn't say!"

He glanced at her sternly. "You could have done a lot of damage by being careless. So could Helen. You both deserved a scare, and you got it."

"Slave driver."

He chuckled, a rare sound that was pleasant in the dark interior of the car. "Next time you'll be more careful, won't you?"

"My job isn't dangerous." She glared at him. "You won't let me do what I really want to," she accused.

"Which is what?" he asked as they stopped at a red traffic light. He laid his arm over the back of the seat and looked into her eyes. "Sleep with me?"

"Of all the conceit," she gasped.

He smiled at her. "You want me."

She averted her eyes. "The light's green."

"Change the subject," he invited as he pulled ahead. "But you'd better stay out of my bed at night," he said matter-of-factly. "It won't do any good to plead with me," he added when she opened her mouth. "My bedroom door will be locked, in case you feel like trying it for yourself."

She stared at him, dumbfounded. He didn't sound like the all-business detective she knew.

He arched an eyebrow. "Sorry to disappoint you," he said. "I'm just not modern enough for casual affairs."

"Dane, do you feel all right?"

"Yes, and don't come an inch closer to see for yourself how I feel," he cautioned sternly. "You can keep your hands off my leg. I'm not that kind of man."

She burst out laughing as his words finally got through to her. She hadn't realized he even had a sense of humor. Presumably, he'd kept it hidden over the years.

"I feel absolutely dangerous," she mused.

"Most women are," he agreed. "I'd put sex-starved virgins at the top of the list, too."

"I'm not that!" she protested.

"How do you know?" He pulled into the parking lot of his own apartment complex. Since most of his business was in Houston, it took too long to commute back and forth from the ranch, so he maintained an apartment in town. He glanced at her as he parked the car. "These urges tend to creep up on women like you. One minute you're blushing and nervous. The next, you're panting and ripping a helpless man's clothes off."

Her eyes twinkled with laughter. "I promise to control my...urges," she assured him.

"God, I hope so. And no peeking when I'm in the shower," he added darkly.

The repartee took all the fear out of the new experience. She followed him up to his second-floor apartment without a qualm.

The room he gave her was decorated in blues, from wallpaper to carpet to curtains. She felt right at home, as she had at the ranch. All it needed was Beryl fussing over them.

"I'll cook, if you like," she volunteered. "I love it."

"No argument from me," he nodded. "I can cook, but I hate it."

She opened the freezer. It was well stocked. So was the refrigerator. "How about a steak and salad for supper?"

"Suits me." He kicked off his shoes and collapsed on the sofa with his jacket half-off.

She went into the guest room and changed into jeans and a sweatshirt, walking around in socks but no shoes. He was apparently as shoes-prejudiced as she was, because he left his off, too.

When she got back to the kitchen, he was out of his jacket and tie, his shirt half-unbuttoned down the front. She studied him covertly, curious about his body in a way she never had been about any other man's. His chest, what she could see of it, was covered in thick black hair. He was deeply tanned from his face down to what she could see of the taut muscular flesh above his belt buckle, and it didn't look like the type of coloring gotten from the sun.

"It's natural," he murmured, surprising her by reading the question in her eyes. "I tan in the summer, but this stays with me year-round. One of my grandfathers was Spanish."

"I didn't mean to stare."

He took the package of steaks out of her hands and tossed it to one side. His lean hands tugged until she fell against him. In his reclining posture against the counter, the contact was total, all the way up and down, and she stiffened unconsciously.

"No surprises," he promised. "Just this. Watch." His voice was deep and sensuous. He held her waist loosely with one hand while the other slowly worked buttons out of buttonholes and finally tugged his shirt free of his slacks, disclosing a broad, muscular chest that was almost completely camouflaged by thick, curling black hair. "Now, look at me," he said quietly.

She did, helplessly. She'd never seen anyone quite as masculine or as sensuous. He even smelled male, a scent that worked on her senses fiercely as she stood against his long, powerful legs and stared at the expanse of bare flesh he'd uncovered for her.

"Your eyes are very expressive," he said, his eyes darkening, glittering. "Giving away secrets."

"What kind of secrets?" she asked huskily, lifting her face to meet that hungry gaze.

"You'd be surprised." He bent and bit at her mouth roughly. The contact was swift, and then she was free. "Keep those sultry eyes to yourself. They're more dangerous than you realize."

He moved lazily toward the bedroom. Tess had barely recovered her balance and her good sense by the time he'd changed into tight jeans and a white T-shirt. The clothing fit him like a second skin, outlining a body that most men would have killed for. He was tall, but not thin. His broad shoulders tapered down in a wedge, over a muscular chest to lean hips and impossibly long legs. He was built like a rodeo rider. Tess had to drag her gaze back to the steaks.

"Like coffee?" he asked, smiling with pure delight at the way she was watching him.

"Yes."

"I'll make it."

The kitchen was too small for two people. That was probably why, she thought breathlessly, he was constantly brushing against her in the most arousing way as he brewed the coffee.

He finished, but he didn't go away. In his sock feet, he was still taller than she was, and his relaxed manner of dress made her much too aware of him as a man.

"I disturb you," he mused.

She started to deny it, then thought better of that. He might be compelled to prove it if she did. "Yes," she said instead.

He leaned back on his hands against the counter, smiling with his eyes in a way that made her knees weak.

"Why don't you come over here and do something about it," he challenged softly.

She wanted to groan. She shouldn't have been vulnerable. The last time she'd been in this apartment, he'd hurt her, scarred her, almost savaged her. How could she feel so wanton now?

"Dane," she protested, her eyes lifting to his.

"I can feel you tremble," he whispered deeply, his eyes narrowing with desire. "I can hear you breathing, Tess." His eyes fell to her breasts, which were shuddering under the thick sweatshirt. "Think how it would be, if I eased up the hem of that sweatshirt and slid my lips over your breasts, took the nipple in my mouth and made it tight and hard...."

"Dane!"

She was shaking. She barely saw him move the frying pan off the burner and turn off the stove. His lean hand snaked out and caught her wrist, pulling her within reach. Both hands went to the sweatshirt and bunched it, clutched it, while his dark eyes probed hers.

"Inch by inch," he whispered, moving it up to her rib cage. "Inch by aching inch, with my hands on your bare skin..."

Her face burned. Her body burned. She gave in quite suddenly, closing her eyes with a shaky breath, arching her back to ease his way. She felt his hands spread over her rib cage, warm and faintly rough, as he pushed the fabric up farther. He bent and she felt the hot moistness of his lips touch her. She shivered and moaned harshly, her voice unrecognizable.

"Lean on me so that you don't fall," he whispered. His tongue eased out against her bare flesh, teasing it, spreading over it until she shuddered, the hem of the sweatshirt rising with his hands to the very edge of her breast in its soft

icy casing. His nose rubbed against the lower band of the
ra and she clutched at his shoulders to keep her balance, so
verwhelmed that tears of tense pleasure were stinging her
yes.

She hung, waiting, yielding, totally submissive to any-
hing he wanted to do to her. Waited . . . waited . . .

"Tess!" His voice exploded into the silence. His hands
ontracted suddenly and his head jerked up while he fought
or breath. "My God, I'm sorry . . . !"

He pulled the sweatshirt down and left the kitchen with-
ut looking at her. She couldn't move for several long sec-
nds. She was dimly aware of water running somewhere, but
ven that didn't immediately register. She finally managed
o stand up and turn her attention back to the steaks. They
were done, but not burned, thank God. She put them on a
latter with shaking hands.

She'd set the table, served the food, and poured the cof-
ee by the time he rejoined her. He was wearing a shirt over
is T-shirt now, and it was buttoned. His hair was damp, as
f he'd just come from a shower. Probably he had. She
vouldn't have minded some cold water, either. She was still
n fire for him. Incredible, that kind of hunger, when only
lays before she'd been afraid of him.

"It's all right," he said quietly, noticing the way she
voided looking directly at him while they ate. "Nothing
iappened."

Nothing? She almost said the word aloud. She couldn't
nanage to look at him. Not that he was paying her any at-
ention. His eyes, like his mind, were forcibly concentrated
n his steak.

"This is good," he said. "I can't ever get it medium rare.
Either it's raw or leather."

"It's the heat," she faltered. "You have to be sure the
an's hot enough."

"You can teach me, while you're here."

"Yes, all right."

He looked at her then, finally, his eyes dark and oddly wary. "Why so embarrassed, Tess?" he asked quietly. "I didn't even touch you intimately."

"You did," she protested. "With words..."

His expression was unreadable. Intense and faintly threatening. "Things went too far, too fast. I was playing with you," he said cruelly. "Until you melted into me like that..."

Her heart felt as if he'd kicked it. Perhaps that was how he meant it to sound. "I get the message," she said, forcing her voice to sound light and unconcerned. She looked up, surprising an odd expression on his face as he stared at her. "I'm as guilty as you are."

He leaned back in his chair, his coffee cup in his hand as he looked at her openly. "Fair enough. But before you get any ideas about why it happened, it's mostly abstinence, Tess," he said tautly. "I haven't been intimate with a woman since the shooting. Maybe I'm more desperate than I realized."

So that was it. Hope died hard, but he was forcing her to realize that it wasn't undying love that had motivated him. All the same, he puzzled her. She couldn't stop the question slipping out. "Why hasn't there been a woman?" she asked.

He stared at her, shocked. "Because of my leg," he said involuntarily.

"Because it's still painful?"

"Because of the way it looks. The way *I* look, with my leg shot to pieces." He frowned. "And maybe because of you," he added reluctantly, searching her eyes. "Sex...hasn't appealed to me much since you ran from me that day." He averted his eyes. "Call it a lack of self-confidence."

"You were different then," she began slowly. "To-night..."

Well, you didn't frighten me at all.''

"So I noticed," he said tersely. He stared at her until she blushed. "Don't trust me, Tess. If I'd gotten my mouth as far as your breasts, I honestly don't know what would have happened. Do you understand, little one?" he asked, his eyes narrow with concern. "I want you. God, Tess, I want you so damned much!" he whispered huskily.

It was true. She'd gotten under his skin in the past few days. He'd never been as tender, or as aroused, in his entire life as he'd been with her lately. Her responsiveness went to his head, made him careless and vulnerable.

"But you don't want to, do you?" she asked softly. She searched his dark eyes.

"You're a virgin," he said stiffly. "You tell me if I want to."

He was more open than he'd ever been. It was obvious that he was afraid of commitment, of loving, of being deserted again. He didn't trust women, or like them. But his body was starved for physical satisfaction, and Tess was innocent and handy. She had to keep the situation in perspective.

"If I weren't innocent—" she began.

"If you weren't, we'd already be lovers," he said heavily. "You're afraid of me like that, but you want me just the same." His dark eyes narrowed on her flushed face. "The first time might be pretty uncomfortable," he said, his voice almost choked with feeling. "I might not be able to help hurting you, since it's been so long for me. But the second time..." His high cheekbones went ruddy as he looked at her. "The second time, I'd pleasure you until you cried. I'd be tender. So tender. I'd love you the way I just did in the kitchen, slowly and softly. I'd put my lips all over you. And by the time I joined your body to mine in that intimate way, you'd be sobbing under my mouth...."

He cursed under his breath and got up, running a rough hand over his face. "God," he breathed unsteadily. "I've got to get out of here!"

Tess watched him leave the room, trembling with desire that he'd kindled so unexpectedly. She could hardly believe that he wanted her so much. All the years he'd denied it, been hostile, kept her at arms' length had been a sham. With shocking clarity, she saw right through him to the vulnerability he was trying to hide. He cared. He cared deeply. Maybe he always had, and her reaction to his ardor had hurt him. She hadn't known anything about him, really. Hadn't totally understood that he'd been savaged by two women he cared about, persecuted by one and deserted in his time of need by the other. He was afraid to love, but he did. Tess caught her breath. He loved her. It was the only possible explanation for the way he was with her lately, for the tenderness that he was learning to give her, for his protective attitude.

He didn't know it, or wouldn't admit it. But the realization made Tess feel warm all over. The trick was going to be making sure he didn't find out that she knew. In the meantime, her heart almost burst with joy. He was hers; he belonged to her now as surely as if he'd given her a solemn vow.

He came back a few minutes later, smoking a cigarette and looking totally uninvolved.

"Want some more coffee?" she asked gently.

"Please."

She poured it while he watched her, averting his eyes when she noticed. They drank coffee in tense silence.

"I'll get used to having you here," he said after a minute, "and we'll manage. I can't let you go home until the dealers are caught and the court decides how to dispose of them."

"I know. I'll try not to be too much trouble," she added with a smile. She got up and brought out a pudding she'd made for dessert, serving it with no conversation at all. When he touched her, he was vulnerable. But the minute he moved away, the wall came back, reinforced. Except that now she knew why he kept building it, and she wasn't hurt by it anymore.

Dane was fighting his feelings tooth and nail. He could go crazy for her if he let himself. That couldn't be. Tess was an old-fashioned girl, with old-fashioned ideas about life and men, courtesy of her grandmother, who'd been responsible for most of her upbringing. He couldn't take her to bed and forget about her. So he had to forget about her physically. In order to accomplish that, as much as he hated to, he was going to have to push her away and keep her there.

He studied her downcast face with eyes that wanted her, but he averted his gaze the minute she looked up. Boss and employee, he told himself. Surely he could manage that.

Five

Tess enjoyed living with Dane. She hadn't expected it to be so sweet, even just being with him while they watched television at night. He liked to sit around in his white T-shirts and jeans, in his sock feet, and sprawl over his armchair while he drank beer and watched old movies. Tess found herself relaxing with him, now that she had a good idea how he felt about her. The way he watched her was exciting, like the evasive tenderness in his eyes when she smiled at him.

He was a loner by nature, a very private man with any number of hang-ups that she discovered quite by accident. It embarrassed him to discuss his feelings, so he never let conversation between them get personal. They talked about the job, about everything except themselves.

A few days after she'd moved in, she was watching a program about birth. He came into the room during it, having been working in his study.

As if it disturbed him to see the embryo being shown at that moment on the screen, he turned to leave.

"I can change the channel if you don't want to watch this," she offered.

He hesitated, his eyes going reluctantly back to the screen. They were showing a delivery room now, a very explicit delivery.

"Sorry." She pushed the Off button on the remote control and laid it down. "I was curious," she confessed. "I never learned much about sex and reproduction at home, and school courses are very brief. I wanted to know how babies . . . how they grew."

"How they got made, you mean," he corrected, watching her face color. "But they didn't show that, did they?"

She cleared her throat. "Not really."

"I've got a book," he said slowly. "You wouldn't want to read it with me here, I know, but you might find it interesting. It shows how people make love without being graphic or offensive."

Her eyes searched his averted face. "I didn't think men were curious about things like that. I mean, you know it all already, don't you?"

He lit a cigarette, pausing in the doorway. "I know how to have sex with a woman," he corrected. "I . . . wanted to know how to make love."

The words made her warm inside. He looked frankly embarrassed. She watched him quietly. "Because I ran from you?"

His eyes glowered at her. "Don't get personal."

She smiled. "That was why, though, wasn't it?"

He drew in an irritated breath and took another draw from the cigarette. "Maybe it was. So what?" he asked belligerently. "It isn't as if I'll ever need to know for your sake. I'm not going to make love to you."

Her eyes fell to the irregular rise and fall of his broad chest. "I wouldn't be afraid of it now," she said softly. "You're very sexy. I didn't want you to stop that time in the kitchen."

His heart shuddered in his chest. "Talking like this is dangerous," he whispered. "You don't know how dangerous."

She looked up at him, her eyes adoring his lean, hard face. "Dane, have you ever thought about having a child?" she asked huskily.

His face exploded with color. He moved jerkily and turned away from her to pull nervously at his cigarette. "No," he said curtly.

"You don't want children?" she persisted.

He fingered the cigarette, staring at its glowing orange tip with eyes that barely saw it. "It wouldn't have made any difference, Tess," he said after a minute. He looked down at her, his expression reluctant. "I can't father a child."

Her mind wouldn't absorb it. She heard the words without comprehending them.

He turned, his eyes dark and quiet as they searched hers. "Jane wanted to get pregnant," he said slowly. "She was obsessed with it. Maybe that's why I couldn't be gentle with her. She demanded, raged at me when she didn't conceive. I felt like some gelded bull by the time she gave up and stopped offering herself to me." He sighed wearily. "I couldn't make her pregnant. Eventually, I couldn't even make love properly." He bent over to put out the cigarette, only half-smoked. "You think you've got scars because of what I did to you. I wish you could see mine."

He turned and started to leave.

She got up, too, and went to him, her eyes big and soft. "There are a lot of reasons why women don't conceive."

"She had a child by her new husband barely ten months after they married," he said curtly.

"That wasn't what I meant. You like jeans, but they create a climate that sometimes prevents men from being fertile...." She flushed as she realized what she was saying.

He lifted an eyebrow. "You're a virgin, I believe?"

"That program I was watching mentioned it," she hedged.

"I don't wear jeans all the time," he reminded her.

"Well..."

His gaze went slowly down her body and back up. She was wearing jeans herself, with a floppy, button-up green shirt. Her hair was up in a disheveled knot on top of her head. She looked young and pretty and very sexy.

"Go away," he said softly. "If I touch you, I won't stop. I can't stop. I'll go every inch of the way."

She searched his eyes and the flush got worse. It was as intimate as a kiss, the way she looked at him. "I know, Dane," she breathed.

His jaw tautened. His breathing changed suddenly, sharply.

She looked down, and her eyes triggered a reaction he'd been trying desperately to avoid. She didn't look away, even then. She found him fascinating. Her expression told him so.

"You're afraid of me," he reminded her with choked passion in his voice. "Hold that thought."

"If you were gentle, I wouldn't be afraid," she said. She lifted her eyes to his and searched them, her body tingling with new sensations, new needs. He loved her. She knew it all the way to her bones, and if she could let him see how it would be with someone who cared, really cared about him, he might change his mind about commitment.

He was sure he was going to die from what he was feeling. He felt near to bursting with it.

Tess felt his tension, sensed how limited his control was. It wouldn't she thought, recklessly, take very much to break through his restraint.

In fact, it didn't. She took one step toward him, and his will collapsed.

He bent and picked her up, managing her slight weight easily, even with his bad back. He didn't look at her as he carried her into his bedroom and kicked the door shut.

He placed her in the center of his bed and stood over her, looking down at the soft contours of her body, his face like rock.

Her hands were beside her head on the beige coverlet, her lips parted, her eyes yielding and submissive, like her body.

"It will hurt," he said tersely.

"I know," she whispered.

His hands trembled as he took off his T-shirt and dropped it onto the floor. He stood, fighting for control. "If you change your mind after I've touched you, I won't be able to stop," he said hoarsely. "Don't you understand?"

"I love you, Richard," she whispered, using the name he never let anyone use, the name she'd always wanted to call him because nobody else did. "I love you with all my heart. I never stopped, even when I was scared to death of you."

He winced. "Tess . . . !"

"Teach me. Love me," she said gently.

His eyes closed. His fists clenched at his sides and he shuddered visibly. "I don't want this to happen," he ground out. "God in heaven, you're a virgin . . . !"

"I love you," she whispered again.

He looked at her, his face quietly resigned as he registered the enormity of the gift she was offering him. "I'll try to give you tenderness," he said slowly. "If not at first, afterwards. I won't . . . hurt you deliberately, you understand?"

"Yes."

He sat down and leaned over her, his eyes moving possessively down her relaxed body. He touched her lips with a tentative brush of his fingers, an action that made her ripple with pleasure.

"There is no more precious gift than what you're offering me," he said huskily. "You can only give your chastity once."

"Shouldn't it belong to someone I love more than my own life?" she asked gently.

He framed her face with unsteady hands. "I...can't love you," he said bitterly. "Tess..."

Her fingers touched his mouth. She knew that he was denying how he felt out of fear. The very hesitancy in his actions told her more than words could how much he cared for her.

"I won't ask you for anything," she promised. "Not even for you to love me. I want to belong to you completely, just this once. I want to know how it feels with someone I love."

He bent to her lips, stumped for words. His mouth trembled as it settled on hers. He opened it, gently, and his hands slid under her nape, to lift her face, tilt it to the gentle assault of his mouth and then his tongue.

Tess smiled under the slow loving as his lips whispered over her face, learning its contours, so tender that they made her warm all over.

His hands slid down, under her back, and he lay down beside her, lazily bringing her body to his as he slid one long leg between both of hers and began to kiss her with slow hunger.

She tangled her hands in his thick, cool hair and drifted while his hands found their way under her blouse, against the soft skin of her back. He kissed her until her mouth was gently swollen, then carefully unfastened the bra so that he could caress her breasts. Their hard tips dragged abrasively against his palms and she began to breathe raggedly as his expert touch kindled fires within her.

"I've never looked at you, even if I have touched you like this before," he whispered, his hands coming back to the buttons that secured the shirt. "Now I'm going to."

She sat up while he divested her of everything she wore above the waist. But when she started to lie back down, his hands prevented her.

He held her there, his lips teasing hers while his knuckles played with exquisite tenderness against her taut nipples. She shivered, and he lifted his head to look at her eyes.

"This is exciting," he said unsteadily. "I've never done this."

"Neither have I," she confessed.

"I want you... in my mouth, Tess," he whispered jerkily, bending his head.

She arched back over his arms as he opened his mouth on her breast and began a warm, moist suction against the nipple. It was like flying, she thought shakily. She felt a burst of heat in her lower body, a surge of ecstasy that startled a cry from her lips.

"Yes," he said, nuzzling the softness his mouth was exploring. "Yes, little one."

She went from plateau to plateau in the minutes that followed, so dazed and helpless from pleasure that she lay almost lifeless while he removed her clothes. Then she watched him take off his own, afterwards noticing the way he hesitated with his back to her.

"It won't... matter," she said, her voice thick and unsteady as she realized why he was hesitating. She could see the deep scar the bullets had left near his spine. She knew there were worse ones on his chest. "I love you!"

He turned. Her eyes went to the core of his masculinity with awe and wonder before they reluctantly moved to his scarred chest and shoulder and leg. There were white streaks and an area that was graphic evidence of a shooting, but to Tess, who loved him, they were only faint imperfections in a body that nature couldn't have improved on.

She shifted on the coverlet, a tiny movement of her hips, her long legs, as she looked up into his eyes and shivered. Woman at the mercy of man and her own aching need of him.

"You are the most beautiful human being I've ever seen," he said hoarsely, his eyes on her body.

"So are you," she whispered.

He eased down beside her, trembling from his years of abstinence and his raging hunger for this one woman. "I want you, baby," he whispered against her warm belly, feeling her jerk under its intimate touch. "Feel how much."

He slid over her, against her, while his lips touched hers in tender teasing, his powerful, hair-roughened body hard and sensually abrasive against hers as he drew it over her trembling warmth. The evidence of his need was blatant and awesome.

"Let me fill you," he whispered at her open mouth. He positioned her carefully as his tongue teased around her lips and slowly, slowly, past her teeth into the soft, sweet darkness of her mouth. "Open your mouth... for me."

Incredible, she thought in the flash of blind pain that accompanied the words and his slow movement. Incredible, that he could make her want him so much....

His lean hand was on her thigh, curling around it, pulling her upward. It contracted, but what she felt was his tongue sliding into her mouth, the fullness of it warm and welcome. The pain came again and she shivered.

"I'm sorry that I have to hurt you like this," he breathed, nibbling at her mouth. He lifted his head and looked into her eyes. His were dark as night, blazing, glazed. His hand contracted again and pulled. "Let me watch you become a woman," he whispered, his eyes holding hers as he slowly pushed his hips down against hers.

Her nails curled into his shoulders and she gasped, shuddering.

"Tell me," he whispered huskily as he moved. "Share it with me."

"It . . . burns," she choked. "Like . . . fire!"

His breath was hot in her mouth as he looked at her and moved again. "Don't cry, little one," he said huskily. "Only a few more seconds . . ."

She moaned and shivered. His remorseful eyes held hers and he took a long, shaky breath. His hand contracted. "You're going to fight me now, because it's going to hurt like hell. But I have to finish it," he whispered, and the muscles in his hips bunched. His eyes dilated as he felt the barrier give. His face flushed with the knowledge, even as he heard her cry out and saw her eyes dilate with pain.

He didn't stop. She pushed at him frantically, but he didn't stop. Her head went back and she sobbed. Then, when she thought she couldn't bear it, the pain all at once eased.

He let out the breath he'd been holding. He didn't move, his body poised against her, his eyes holding hers. He smiled.

Her eyes were bright with tears. He bent and kissed them, sipping the wetness away, his cheek sliding against hers as his lips pressed with aching tenderness all over her face and he whispered husky words of endearment and praise.

Her hands relaxed on his shoulders and her body followed suit. She felt his possession of her increase with the tiny movement and she flushed as she met his eyes.

He smiled tenderly, through his own raging need. "Now I can make love to you, Tess," he said softly. "It won't hurt anymore."

His teeth caught her upper lip and nibbled at it softly as his hips lifted and pushed, lifted and pushed, in a slow, tender rhythm that made her gasp and jerk with sudden, stark pleasure.

He watched her react to it with an excess of male pride. "You were very brave," he whispered as he increased the pressure and rhythm, feeling her body begin to echo his slow movements. "Very, very brave. You didn't even cry out."

"Dane?" she cried, frightened.

"Let me pleasure you," he whispered, bending to her mouth as the silver ripples worked up his spine. "I'll teach you now. I'll teach you, baby."

Instinctively she knew he'd never done this before, never loved anyone the way he was loving her. It was as if he, too, were a virgin all over again. She clung to him, sobbing as he'd promised she would, begging for fulfillment at the last. He gave it to her unexpectedly, completely, lifted his head and watched her convulse, and smiled through his own fierce excitement before it caught him up in its vortex and made him cry out harshly with the sheer joy of ecstasy.

He held her for a long time afterward, drying her tears, kissing her undemandingly, soothing her torn, exhausted body. He got up and got a cold beer from the refrigerator, sharing it with her while he had a cigarette. He wasn't thinking about tomorrow. There was only tonight, only the joy of loving, the beauty of her whispered love for him, the sweet anguish of fulfillment.

He put the half-finished beer on the bedside table, and crushed out his cigarette. Then he eased her over onto her back and slid up beside her.

"I'm going to take you again, now," he whispered as he moved between her long, trembling legs. "This time, it will be very slow, very gentle. This time, you'll feel it so intensely that you'll cry out, as I did earlier."

"I...love you," she whispered frantically, her body so perfectly attuned to his that the first hard thrust of it brought a cry of ecstasy from her parched lips.

"Already?" he asked huskily, moving fiercely against her.

"Now," she groaned. "Now, now, now...!"

He thought that never in his life had he felt such sensations. He convulsed almost immediately, feeling her body surge under him, hearing her hoarse cries as he fulfilled her once, twice, three times. He shouldn't have been capable of this, of endless potency, of tireless arousal. But he was. Perhaps the abstinence, or what he felt for her, or even her unexpectedly sweet sensuality triggered it. Whatever the reason, by the time he finally rolled away from her, too exhausted to even kiss her swollen mouth one last time, he was asleep before his head even reached the pillow.

The next morning, she kissed him awake. He opened his eyes and saw her over him, saw the light in her eyes, and he groaned softly as he levered her instantly onto her back and rolled onto her body.

"No," she whispered quickly, blushing when he loomed over her with virile intent. "I'm sorry," she said miserably. "But it hurts...."

He breathed slowly until he could calm his blood. His hand smoothed over her soft breast. "I took you four times," he whispered, lifting his eyes back to hers. "I hurt you."

"No," she said, shaking her head. "Oh, no, you didn't hurt me."

He brushed his lips over hers, and then over her eyes. "But I would if we made love now?"

"I'm afraid so."

He sighed and rolled onto his back. "I should have thought about that. I'm not properly awake. Do you want some coffee?"

"Yes. I'll make it."

She started to get up, realized she was undressed, and pulled the sheet demurely to her breasts.

He glanced at her, following her embarrassed gaze to his own body. He made a sound and threw his legs over the side of the bed, carelessly tugging on his briefs and jeans and socks while she watched.

"You can dress while I shave," he said. He didn't look at her.

She watched him with soulful eyes that he didn't see. *I love you,* she wanted to say. But he wouldn't have said it back, even if he had made love to her like a man out of his mind with it. He loved her. She was certain of it now, and her eyes adored him.

"Get a move on," he said from the doorway. "We'll be late for work."

"Oh. Of course."

He didn't mention what had happened. Not by word or inference did he refer to it. He was all business.

Tess had expected resistance. She wasn't surprised by his attitude. He was a man afraid of emotion, and he had every reason to be. He couldn't be sure even of Tess. She knew that, and wasn't offended.

"Helen said I could go with her at lunchtime to that stakeout," she began as they finished toast and coffee.

He glared at her. "No."

"Let me finish, please," she said quietly. "I'm going to be the decoy. While people are watching me, she's going to be following them."

"You'd be too vulnerable," he said shortly. "Helen isn't being stalked by dope peddlers. You are. No, ma'am. You'll be where I can see you, all the time. I'm not trusting you to anyone except me."

She blushed. "All right."

He scowled darkly. "And don't get any ideas about what happened last night. That was a one-off, do you hear me?"

Her eyebrows lifted. "A one-off?" she asked.

His cheeks went ruddy. She looked surprised that he could refer to something so profound in such a way. He was surprised at himself. He glared at her, his heart racing. "What did you expect me to say?" he asked coldly. "That it was the closest I'll get to heaven without dying?"

"Not really," she agreed. "But it was. For me, I mean."

"I hurt you."

Her eyes lifted, searching his. "At first," she agreed. Then she smiled.

His breathing went ragged as the memory of the pleasure they'd shared washed over him. Just looking at her aroused him. He got up from the table, slamming his napkin down. "Let's get out of here," he said roughly.

She went along without an argument, wrapped in acres of dreams and delight because she was loved. He would fight it. That was inevitable. But in the end, he was going to lose. He couldn't resist her any more than she could resist him, but she had to give him time. She couldn't rush him. Not with so much at stake.

Her only regret was that a child couldn't come of the beauty they'd created together. She would have loved a child so much.

Once they got to the office that morning, problems claimed their attention immediately, and for Dane, it seemed to be a relief. He got into the thick of it without a backward glance, leaving Tess to sort out schedules and appointments.

The past few days had been so eventful that Tess had all but forgotten the night she'd been shot. Her arm was a little sore, and it had gotten a workout last night. She flushed and smiled, remembering Dane's mouth on the healed wound. She'd touched his scarred back and shoulder and leg with equal tenderness, stroking it while he made love to her, whispering that it was a badge of honor, a war wound. It had increased the pleasure. She could still hear his voice as he cried out, almost sobbing as the force of ecstasy lifted him over her and shook his powerful body like a whip.

She caught her breath. Could he really believe something that beautiful was only explainable as a "one-off"? She knew better. He did, too, but he'd been hurt so badly that he couldn't accept it just yet.

Her attention was diverted by the telephone, but as the day wore on her body reminded her of the unusual activity it had been subjected to the night before. It was difficult to sit, though she didn't dare mention it in case someone became suspicious.

At lunch, she watched the operatives who were in the office leave; watched with a wistful smile as Helen disappeared. Dane was at a luncheon, so she was in the office alone. He probably hadn't realized she would be by herself when he'd refused to let her go out with Helen for the noon meal. Well, she'd walk up the street to the fast food restaurant and get chicken and biscuits. It was better than nothing.

She put on her coat and locked the office behind her. Her mind was on Dane instead of on where she was going. The sudden shock of a man's hand clamping over her mouth surprised her into stunned immobility.

"Here you are, pretty thing," a rasping voice said harshly. "Right on schedule. When I'm through with you, you won't be in any hurry to tell a jury what you saw!"

Six

Tess couldn't remember ever being quite so afraid. The man had her in a half nelson, and he was slowly dragging her to the front door of the building, where another man was sitting in a running car.

This couldn't be happening, she told herself. She couldn't let it happen. A knife was being held at her ribs, and she felt the certainty of death like black ice on her tongue.

If she let him get her into the car, she didn't have a prayer. She would die. They'd carry her off and then certainly kill her. Desperate men, desperate deeds. The car the other man was driving was an expensive brown sedan, and they were both wearing suits. These were no run-of-the-mill street people, no lower-rank mules. These were men who made millions on the despair and desperation of weak people, and they certainly wouldn't mind killing anyone who stood between them and their livelihood.

Dane had known that. But Tess hadn't realized it until now, when it was too late.

There was a chance, only a brief one, that she might get away before the men got her into the car. When he opened the door at the front of the building, he was certainly going to have to take that knife away from her rib cage for an instant. If she was quick and kept her head, she might get away.

Her heart raced madly. She was shaking all over, but she couldn't give way to panic and fear. She kept telling herself that, going over everything she'd learned from the operatives, the slick little moves they'd taught her about how to get away from a potential attacker. She'd listened and learned. Now those lessons were going to pay off.

She went along with him, acting terrified to throw him off guard. She pleaded with him tearfully to set her free. All the time her mind was working, going over and over the one move she was going to employ when the time came.

It was working. She felt him begin to relax his painful grip. He laughed. He was enjoying her fear. The front door was a foot away. He moved toward it, the knife lifting as he raised his arm to push open the glass door.

Just as he raised it, Tess brought her elbow into his diaphragm with a vicious jab. As his chin came down, she brought the back of her fist up to meet his nose, and felt blood on it. Reacting swiftly, she tore away from him while he was doubled over and ran up the side street toward the crowded main street. It was noon, and people were everywhere. Thank God! The men wouldn't dare risk taking hold of her with a crowd around her. She ran, panting, not daring to look back.

She merged quickly into a group of people waiting for a red light to change. Out of the corner of her eye, she spotted a car speeding up the side street toward her. They wouldn't, she thought feverishly, they wouldn't... !

"Tess!"

She looked. It was a Mercedes, and Dane was at the wheel.

"Dane!" She ran across the side street and scrambled in beside him, throwing her arms around his neck and shivering.

He brought her close for an instant, barely aware of his surroundings in the stark terror he'd just experienced. He'd rushed back to the office, hoping to get there before the operatives left. He'd seen Tess running and the other car suddenly speed away. His choices dwindled immediately to getting to Tess or giving chase. That was no choice at all.

His mouth crushed down over hers for one long instant before he dragged it away and turned the car down the wide street into traffic. He didn't let go of Tess. He couldn't.

"They almost had me," she whispered breathlessly. "One of them grabbed me as I started out of our office. He had a knife at my ribs...."

"God," he groaned harshly, pulling her closer.

"Helen taught me how to defend myself against somebody holding me from behind," she said. Her cheek moved against the soft fabric of his jacket. "I remembered it. I caught him off guard and got away." She grinned, now that it was all over. "It was very exciting," she said, her eyes sparkling as she looked up at him. "I can see why... Dane?"

He pulled off the street into a parking space and sat, white-faced, his hands trembling on the steering wheel. He didn't speak or look at her.

"It's all right," she said softly. She moved, reaching up to draw his head down to hers. She kissed him slowly, nibbling at his lips, his nose, his closed eyes. Her arms slid around him and she pressed close, her face finally sliding against his hot throat and resting there. "It wasn't your fault," she whispered. "You forgot that you'd told me I couldn't go with Helen."

"I didn't forget," he said unsteadily. "I left in plenty of time to get back before the office emptied. But I had a flat on the way."

"Dane?" she murmured.

"Let me hold you, Tess," he said, his voice torn. "Don't talk. Just let me hold you."

She did, sighing as the peace of the embrace finally got through to him and calmed him. He felt guilty, she supposed, although God knew why he should. She didn't blame him. She smiled against his throat and kissed him just below his Adam's apple. She was about to say that for a man who didn't love her, he was certainly excitable. But she thought better of it. He was vulnerable. He wouldn't like having her point it out.

He drew in a rough breath, and she glanced up at him. His eyes were frightening. He touched her face with warm, hard fingers. "Did he hurt you?"

"No," she assured him. Her eyes sparkled. "But I hurt him. I think I broke his nose."

He whistled softly. "I'm going to have to talk to Helen."

"You wouldn't teach me," she said defensively.

"Thank God she did. I'll treat Helen and Harold to the biggest damned anchovy pizzas they can eat," he mused.

"That's nice." She laid her forehead against his chin. "Can I have one, too? I'm hungry."

"Poor little scrap, you haven't eaten." He put her back in her own seat and fastened her seat belt, his hands brushing against her body accidentally and setting her tingling. "You can have a pizza if you want one."

Her eyes melted into his, adoring, acquisitive.

He bridled at that look, at his own vulnerability. He didn't like having her see him when he couldn't hide his disturbed state from her. She might think he was emotionally involved. Ridiculous, of course. All the same . . .

He bent and put his mouth softly over hers, kissing her gently. "From now on, if I have to leave the office, I'll make sure someone's with you. I'm sorry, Tess. Damned sorry."

She smiled. "I told you, it wasn't your fault." She stared at his mouth dizzily. "Kiss me again."

"Too public," he murmured, drawing back. He indicated throngs of passersby.

"We could eat at the apartment, couldn't we?"

"No, we could not," he said gently, reading her expression all too well for his peace of mind. "In the first place, you'll need days to recuperate from what I did to you last night. In the second place," he said, his expression growing sterner by the second, "from now on, you're going to sleep in your own bed, not mine. I won't let that happen again."

"Why not?" she asked softly.

His thumb rubbed slowly over her chin and he looked worried. "Because I don't want commitment," he reminded her. "I won't ever forget how it made me feel to be your first lover. But you want forever after. I don't believe in it anymore. I've had my illusions shattered."

"You might change your mind," she said. "I might grow on you."

"You already have. But I can't marry you," he said bluntly. "Listen to me, Tess. You think you love me, but you don't have any experience of men except what you've learned with me. One day, sex won't be enough for you. You'll want a child."

"I love you, Dane," she said simply.

His cheeks darkened and his eyes seemed to kindle, but he fought down the fever those words initiated. "You don't know what love is," he replied quietly. "You think it's two bodies in bed."

Her eyes searched his. "What we did together last night was much more than two bodies in bed. We made love,

Dane," she said. "Made it so beautifully that I can't imagine ever letting any man but you touch me as long as I live."

His eyes closed. He felt that way, too, but he couldn't tell her. His feelings were locked up, chained.

"It was sex," he said coldly, forcing his eyes to open and stab into hers. "And you're damned lucky I'm sterile or you'd really have a problem."

"I wouldn't have thought so," she said, smiling.

He gazed out the window blindly. "Anyway, it's a moot point," he said. He started the car. "We have to report this to the nearest precinct. Assault with intent is a felony. I'll have that—" he employed some old ranger language "—in jail by sundown, and he won't get out this time, not if I have to call in a few markers and have some old friends help me surround the courthouse!"

She could picture a throng of cold-eyed Texas Rangers holding a courtroom at gunpoint. She laughed gently.

"How can you laugh?" he demanded. "God in heaven, don't you realize how close you came to being killed?"

"Nerves," she told him. "Reaction. Yes, I realize it. I remember thinking I wouldn't see you again," she added, adoring his face with her gray eyes. "It made me sad."

He looked away. He'd had too many shocks lately, all of them to do with losing her. He put the car into gear and pulled out into traffic. He lit a cigarette and didn't say another word all the way to the police station.

Helen gloated later when she found out that Tess had used her instructions to foil a kidnapping. Dane was in a black temper that lasted all day, even if he did unbend enough to give Helen a bonus for teaching Tess how to survive an assault. But he watched Tess openly, his mind on the dope peddlers. He'd never felt so homicidal.

While the office was full of armed operatives, he made his way back to the police station, to talk to the sergeant who was handling the case.

"Nothing yet," Sergeant Graves told Dane when the two men were in the former's office. "We've got feelers out, but those two rats have gone down a hole somewhere. They probably knew we'd pull out all the stops after what they did. Your secretary was damned lucky, do you know that? Tomby, the man who tried to abduct her, got off once on a murder charge for lack of evidence. I don't doubt he'd have killed her if he'd gotten her into his car."

"Neither do I," Dane said stiffly. He didn't want to think about that. He'd go crazy. "I'm volunteering my staff to help find them. I can't risk having Tess at their mercy again."

"We'd appreciate the help," Graves replied. "With your background in police work, you know how much there is to do and how inadequate our staff is. People don't realize the time it takes to run down felons, or the bureaucracy that stands between law enforcement and the justice system."

"God, I do," Dane said heavily. "You try being a ranger. You'll get an eyeful."

The older man smiled wistfully. "I did try. Couldn't pass the oral exam. God, those old-timers are thorough!"

"And damned mean, some of them." Dane chuckled.

"They have to be. Everyone remembers the story of the single Texas Ranger who got off the train after he was called to put down a full-scale riot. The townspeople were astonished that one man was expected to accomplish all that. The ranger just drawled, "Well, you've only got one riot, haven't you?""

"One man was usually enough," Dane replied.

"I've got a hunch about these two men we're after," Graves said suddenly, after the laughter diminished. "They're high-class suppliers. There's a man named Louie on parole for distributing. He has some ties to the same underworld element these two are involved with. I'd like to lean on him a little, unofficially."

Dane smiled slowly. "Got an address?"

The other man returned the smile and scribbled something on a piece of paper. "You don't know where you got this," he cautioned.

Dane nodded as he got to his feet. "It was in my pocket when my jacket came back from the cleaners," he promised.

"Good luck."

"We could both use a little of that."

Back at the office, Dane gave the address to Adams with some instructions. At closing time, he made sure Tess was with him every minute until they got back to his apartment.

He threw off his jacket, an action she watched with possessive familiarity. Living with him had her spoiled. She loved being with him. Once the men who'd assailed her were caught, she'd have to go home. Her face paled at the realization.

He turned, rubbing a hand around the back of his stiff neck, and caught her expression. "What is it?" he asked gently.

"When they catch those two men, I'll have to go home."

He frowned slightly. He didn't want to think about that, either. It made him feel empty. The past few days with her here had been magic, and not just because they'd become lovers. He enjoyed being with her.

"You'll probably be glad," she said, trying to brighten up. "No more lingerie drying in the bathroom, no more shoes under the couch...."

"That isn't quite true," he said. "I'll miss you. I think you'll miss me, too. But we adjusted to being apart a long time ago."

She searched his eyes. "You mean, just after you got shot and I took care of you."

He nodded. "We were almost this close then, until I made a dead set at you and scared you off."

She smiled tenderly. "I'm not scared anymore," she reminded him, and her face colored.

He moved closer, pulling her against him. His head bent over hers and he rocked her gently. "It has to end," he said bitterly. "I told you, I don't want commitment."

Her arms slid under his and she lay her cheek on his broad chest, against his warm white shirtfront. She didn't argue because there was no use. She drew in a breath, savoring every second she had with him. The memories would be sweet, at least. "Can I sleep with you tonight?"

He stiffened. "I want that," he said huskily. "But, no. It will only make it worse when you have to leave."

"That's like not driving a car because it will be irritating when it breaks down."

He chuckled despite himself. "I suppose so." He lifted his head. "It isn't a good idea to get any closer than we already have," he said finally. "It's going to hurt like hell as it is."

She started to speak, but he put his thumb over her lips.

"I know you think you love me," he said. "That will pass, once you're back in your own apartment and resuming your own life. This will seem like a bad dream."

"Last night won't," she replied.

"I know." He kissed her forehead with breathless tenderness. "But it was only one night. You'll forget, in time."

"Will you?"

He let her go and stretched, pretending he didn't hear her. "Who cooks, and what?" he asked. "I feel like a hamburger. Several hamburgers," he amended. "That slice of pizza at lunch wasn't filling."

"Hamburgers it is. I'll cook," she volunteered.

"You always cook. That isn't fair division of labor."

"It is, considering how you cook hamburgers," she said under her breath as she went toward the kitchen.

"Female chauvinism."

"Contradiction in terms."

He made a huffy sound and went into the bedroom to change.

She made hamburgers and sliced some Swiss cheese to go on them, along with chives and onions and mustard and mayonnaise. Dane stared at his suspiciously when she put it before him.

"Try it before you say terrible things about it," she coaxed.

He narrowed one eye and glared at it. Eventually, he picked it up and tasted it, and his eyebrows arched. "Different," he said.

"Kit taught me," she said. "She learned from her boss."

"The office has missed them," Dane said dryly as he washed down bites of hamburger with rich black coffee. "Logan Deverell is one of my biggest accounts. His mother, Tansy, keeps me in the black."

She laughed. "She's a wild woman, isn't she? Always into something, mostly trouble. We spend a lot of time looking for her. Mr. Deverell worries too much."

"Not really," he mused. "Not since she got arrested in Mexico for drug trafficking."

"But she wasn't," she argued. "She bought a colorful purse from a vendor who mistook her for a mule."

"Mistaken identity has landed saner people than Tansy in jail," he reminded her. "If Logan could tie her to a post, he'd stop worrying."

"Yes, but we'd lose his business," she pointed out.

"Perish the thought."

"I miss having lunch with Kit," she sighed. She glanced at him. "She'd have a flying fit if she knew we were living together."

"We aren't," he pointed out.

"We are so. Temporarily, anyway," she replied.

He finished his hamburger and made himself another one. This time he sliced onions and spread mustard on one bun and catsup on another.

"Purist," she muttered.

"I'm conventional," he explained as he sat down again. "I like a downtown hamburger."

She laughed. Her gray eyes sparkled as she looked at him, so enthralled by the sight of him across a table that she couldn't hide it. Even in an old T-shirt and jeans, he was something to see.

"I don't guess we could go down to the ranch for the weekend?" she asked wistfully.

He shook his head, his eyes wary. "We can't risk it."

"Because of the drug dealers." She nodded.

"No, Tess," he replied quietly. "Because we've been lovers. Beryl isn't blind. The way we look at each other would give the show away."

"Oh."

"She's old-fashioned in her attitudes." He grimaced at her blush. "I know. So are you. So am I, for that matter." His eyes darkened. "And despite that, it made me feel ten feet tall to know I was the first. I'll treasure that night as long as I live."

"So will I," she said softly, searching his eyes. "You said you'd never been tender with anyone. But you were patient and gentle, and I know you didn't feel like being that way. You wanted me very badly."

"I wanted to cherish you," he said huskily. "I wanted to give you a sweet memory, something to wipe out the fear I'd kindled in you the first time I kissed you." He shrugged. "Maybe I wanted to know if I was capable of tenderness, as well."

She cleared her throat. "I don't think there's much doubt about that anymore," she said demurely.

His eyes softened as he looked at her. "You were everything I used to dream you would be," he said quietly. "Soft and loving, gently abandoned in my arms. I exhausted you because I couldn't manage to stop. I couldn't get enough of you."

She colored, remembering. She wrapped her hands around her coffee cup and sipped the hot black liquid. She met his eyes evenly. "I'm not sorry," she said. "Not if I died of it, I wouldn't be sorry!"

His jaw tautened. He had to drag his gaze back to his hamburger. He could have said the same to her, but he was getting aroused all over again. "I've got some work to do in the study. Can you amuse yourself?"

"There's a *National Geographic* special on," she replied. "About lizards. I thought I'd watch it."

His eyebrows arched. "Lizards?"

She shrugged. "I don't know why, but I've always been fascinated by them. Especially the Komodo dragons. Have you seen pictures of them? They're huge, and they have forked tongues...."

"And a very well developed Jacobsen's organ," he added, smiling at her surprise. "They interest me, too. So does most wildlife."

"You like cattle and horses. I guess wildlife is wildlife," she mused.

"I'd have liked taking you back to the ranch," he confessed, searching her face quietly. "But Beryl would make you feel uncomfortable."

She looked down at the empty plate. "Is there such a thing as happily ever after these days?" she asked.

"For some people, maybe. I can't forget how my marriage failed, Tess. Maybe it never had a chance, but in the beginning, things were bright for Jane and me. Somewhere along the way, we stopped caring about each other." He looked up. "There aren't any guarantees. If I could give you a child, I might think differently. But I can't. I don't think we could make it work. I'm afraid to take the chance, can you understand that?"

"You think I'm too young," she sighed. Her eyes coveted him shyly. "I don't know whether to be flattered or insulted. I loved you when I was nineteen, and I love you now." She smiled sadly. "How do I stop, Dane?"

His teeth clenched. He couldn't handle questions like that. He swallowed the last of his coffee and put the mug down. "Leave the dishes," he said as he rose. "I'll take care of them, since you did the cooking."

"I don't mind...."

"This is my apartment," he reminded her coolly. "I'm used to doing dishes. And cooking. I've lived alone for years."

He went off in the general direction of the study and she got up after a minute and cleared things away.

"You really must feel like you have a shadow," Helen remarked a couple of days later at work. "Dane never takes his eyes off you, and if he has to be out of the office, it's Adams or me or Nick. You poor thing, I know you'll be glad when this is finally over. Living with Dane must be pure hell. It's a good thing you don't have a social life, or you'd be screaming."

Tess controlled her expression, just barely. "I suppose so."

"Dane would have been your stepbrother, wouldn't he?" Helen asked. "Everyone knows that your respective parents were going to be married. I don't suppose it feels funny to you at all, being that close to him. After all, he's almost family."

She murmured her agreement, but it was a lie. Dane wasn't family. He was the light of her life, except that she wanted something he didn't. She wanted marriage and togetherness. Dane was afraid that she'd turn out like Jane, harping on his inability to make her pregnant, making his life hell.

She wouldn't, though. It was a disappointment, surely, that he couldn't give her a child, but it wasn't the end of the world. She cared about him too much. If it could be only the two of them for fifty years, she'd have leaped at the chance. She couldn't bear to even think of how life was going to be without him, now that she'd known him so intimately.

He didn't seem to be having similar problems. If he was worried about their relationship, his expression gave nothing away. In the evenings, he was pleasant and kind, but he never looked at her too long or came too close. He spent most of his time in his study, working, and when he wasn't in there, he was in bed.

Tess was alone these days at the apartment, and the distance between Dane and herself was growing. He was determined to put her out of his mind. She fought to keep the wonderful closeness they'd attained, but she did it with no help from him.

"Tess, come in here a minute, please," he said the next morning, motioning her into his office.

Nick Reed was in there, too, tall and blond and carelessly attractive. He was Helen's brother, an ex-FBI agent whom Dane had coaxed away from the government agency, and if Tess hadn't been so hopelessly in love with Dane, she'd have gotten weak-kneed every time she saw Nick. He had that kind of good looks. He smiled at her as she sat down on the sofa and waited for Dane to close the door.

"We're going to force their hand," Dane told her abruptly. "Nick's been to see a man I got a tip about. He got some information we can use, and I had him deposit a few clues about your movements in the process. We're going to set you up, honey, and let the bad boys come after you."

"Thanks," she sighed. "I always knew you loved me, really."

Nick chuckled at what he thought was a joke. Dane didn't. His face closed up.

"You'll be quite safe," Dane told her. "We're going to back you to the hilt, the whole damned staff and two off-duty cops. It's the only way I've been able to find that wouldn't give them the advantage. We can't sit and wait until they try for you again. It's too dangerous."

"What do you want me to do?" she asked calmly.

"First they shoot you, then they try to nab you, and you break free and evade them," Nick murmured. "Pity Dane won't let you on the staff, Tess, you're a natural."

"Tell him, tell him," she muttered, pointing at Dane. "He thinks I'm hopeless at detective work."

"Getting shot doesn't require ability as a detective," Dane informed her.

"No, but getting away from a potential killer does," Nick told him. "Some of our best operatives wouldn't have been able to manage—"

"Let's keep to the topic at hand," Dane said tersely, glaring at Nick. "Tess, this is what we want to do," he began.

He told her when, where and how they were going to set the trap. She was afraid and nervous, but she reminded herself that she'd been both when she evaded the men in the first place. She could keep her head under fire. She knew that now. It would be all right.

At least she'd be out of danger when it was over. She'd be out of Dane's life, too. He seemed to be in a hurry to accomplish that, even if she wasn't. What did they say about a quick cut being kindest in the long run? Maybe she could get her life back together when she was out of Dane's, but she'd never be the same without him. Nothing was going to change that.

That weekend at the apartment, Dane was unusually restless. He couldn't sit still long enough to watch television.

"Let's go out," he said tersely, glancing at her. "Put something on."

"I've got something on," she began, indicating her jeans and T-shirt.

"Then add a jacket and some sneakers to it. I feel like riding."

"Where?"

"At the ranch," he muttered. He saw her flush. "It's Beryl's day off," he told her. "Even so, we manage the facade in public. Helen actually asked me if I'd ease up on you. She thinks I've been giving you hell."

"Haven't you?" she asked pertly.

He turned away. "Come on. Sitting around here all day isn't going to do a thing for us."

Probably not, since he wouldn't touch her, she thought bitterly. But a whole day in his company wasn't anything to sneer at. In the years to come, every minute would be a precious memory.

She grabbed her denim jacket, slipped into her pink sneakers and followed him out the door.

It was a cool day, and she was glad of the jacket when she and Dane rode across the lower part of his ranch, which lay along the boundary of the Big Spur. Her efforts to get on the horse had amused Dane, bringing a rare smile to his lips. The old mare he'd given her to ride was gentle, though, and after a while she felt quite at home on the animal. It wasn't nearly the ordeal she'd thought it would be, learning how to ride. She was enjoying it.

She stared curiously at the red-coated cattle in the distance.

"They're the same color as yours," she remarked, nodding toward them. "Are they the same breed?"

"Santa Gertrudis," he agreed. He eased back in the saddle, grimacing a little.

"Is your back all right?" she asked with concern.

He glance at her with a wry smile. "It was until a few nights ago."

She actually gasped out loud.

He chuckled helplessly. "My God."

"Do you mind?" she asked breathlessly, her color flaring.

"My back is all right," he assured her "A little stiff, but it gets that way from routine work. I can assure you," he added in a soft tone, "that I'd much rather have a stiff back from what we did together than from going on stakeout."

She cleared her throat. "I see."

"Coward. You were the one who brought it up last time." He caught her hand in his and brought it to his mouth. "Thank you for the gift you gave me that night."

She really colored then. She couldn't manage words.

He stopped his horse, and hers, and clasped her hand against him until she looked his way.

"I felt like a whole man," he said slowly. "Even if I couldn't give you a child."

She winced. "Dane, a child isn't the only reason two people marry."

"Perhaps not," he said wearily. "But it can destroy a marriage." His face went hard. "God knows, it destroyed mine."

"I'm not Jane!" she cried.

He looked at her hungrily. "There's no doubt about that," he said quietly. "She could barely suffer having me in bed." His high cheekbones went ruddy. "You didn't, though. My God, you..." He couldn't even find the words. He pressed his mouth hard into her palm, his eyes closed on an anguished scowl. "I've never had it like that," he said in a rough tone.

She flushed, too, at the unfamiliar emotion in his deep voice. "I thought it was always good for the man."

His dark eyes caught hers. "I all but passed out in your arms," he said huskily. "Just thinking about how it was arouses me."

Her lips parted. It aroused her, too. She sensed his vulnerability, and just for an instant she thought he might be weakening.

The sudden sound of approaching horses distracted him, too soon. He let go of her hand and his eyes narrowed under the wide brim of his hat.

"Two peas in a pod," he mused, watching two tall riders approach.

Tess shaded her eyes. "Who are they?"

"Cole Everett and King Brannt." He kicked his boot out of the stirrup and looped his leg around his saddle horn while he lit a cigarette. He grinned as the two men galloped up beside him and stopped. He knew they'd seen him with Tess and had moved in for a better look. It was, as they knew, unusual for him to bring a woman to the ranch.

"Nice day," the older of the two remarked, his narrow silvery eyes appraising Tess's flushed face.

"Good weather, too," the other man agreed, his dark eyes twinkling in a lean, formidable countenance.

"Her name is Teresa Meriwether," Dane told them with exaggerated patience. "Tess for short. Her father was going to marry my mother until the wreck, so she's . . . family. She's my secretary at the agency."

Cole Everett pushed back his creamy Stetson and eyed Dane curiously, his silver eyes quiet and steady. "Do tell."

He glanced at Tess. "Nice to meet you," he said, smiling. He had a warm smile, not sarcastic or mocking.

"Same here," King Brannt agreed. He was pleasant enough, but he had a cutting edge to his personality that intimidated Tess. She smiled shyly in his direction, wondering absently how his Shelby had ever gotten up enough nerve to marry such a wildcat.

Everett, too, had an untamed look, but he was older than the other two men, graying at the temples.

"How's Heather?" Dane asked Cole. "Still teaching voice?"

"And writing songs," Cole replied. "She sold one last year to a group called Desperado, based up in Wyoming, and their lead singer won another Grammy with it. Heather was over the moon. So were our boys." He chuckled. "They're just at the age where they like pop music."

"My kids like it, too," King mused. "Dana's got a keyboard and Matt has drums." He held a hand to his ear. "Shelby spends a lot of time working in the kitchen garden while they practice. They're all in high school. His three hang out with my two," he muttered, glaring at Cole. "God knows, I'll go insane one day and start howling at the moon from the noise."

"I send them over to his house so that we can have some peace and quiet at ours," Cole explained dryly. "Shelby told Heather that she wished she had more than two kids of her own." He pursed his lips at King. "You aren't too old yet, are you?"

"Speak for yourself, Grandpa," King returned. He glanced at Dane curiously. "Ever think of marrying again?" he asked bluntly.

Dane didn't bat an eyelash. "No. Anything in particular you wanted, besides a look at my houseguest?" he added with a meaningful stare.

"We could use a new bull," Cole reminded him. "King's got one he's ready to sell, and he needs a new one of his own. Since you and I are ready to unload . . . er, sell . . . that bull of ours, King thought we might work out a trade, when you've got time to discuss it." He grinned at Tess, ignoring King's dry glance in his direction. "Not today, of course."

Dane chuckled at the blatant excuse. He saw right through them. "Okay," he said. "I'll come over next weekend and we'll talk about it." By then, he thought, he'd have sprung the trap on Tess's assailant and she'd have moved out. The thought depressed him.

"Suits us," King said. "As for unloading your bull on me," he added with a mocking smile at Cole Everett, "that'll be the day."

"You watch too many reruns of old John Wayne movies," Cole pointed out. "You're starting to sound like the character he played in *The Searchers.*"

The younger man cocked an eyebrow. "All the same, you won't slip a worn-out bull under my nose."

Cole looked insulted. "Would I do that to a business partner?"

"Sure," King said pleasantly. "Like you tried to land me with that gelding last year when I wanted a new stallion for my stud."

"It wasn't my fault. I swear to God I had no idea he'd been to the vet—"

"Like hell you didn't. He was in on it with you," he added, nodding toward Dane. "You gave it away when you started snickering into your hat."

"Yes, but the joke backfired, didn't it?" King mused. "I bought the animal anyway and he turned out to be one of the best stud horses I've got. The vet pulled a fast one on both of *you.*"

Tess was laughing out loud by now. "I thought you people were friends!" she burst out.

"Oh, we are," King agreed. "But friends are much more dangerous than enemies."

"I'll drink to that," Dane murmured.

"Yes, well, it pays not to turn your back on these two," Cole returned. "Are you staying at the ranch long? Heather would enjoy getting to meet you, I'm sure. I imagine your job is pretty interesting. *He* never talks about it." He jerked a thumb toward Dane.

"That's how *he* keeps his clientele," Dane returned easily. "We're leaving in a few minutes, but maybe I'll bring her over another time."

"You do that. Well, we'll see you next weekend, then."

"Nice to have met you," King added to Tess. He wheeled his mount and started up. Cole Everett smiled and followed suit.

Tess watched them ride away. "Have your friends been married a long time?"

"Years and years," he replied. "Their kids are all in their early teens now." *Kids.* His face hardened. "We'd better get back."

She put her hand on his upper arm as he gathered the reins in one lean hand. "Don't let it wear on you like that," she said softly. "Dane, children aren't everything...."

"They are if you can't produce any," he said tersely. He looked into her eyes with pure malice. "Tell me you don't want a baby, Tess," he challenged coldly.

Her eyes clouded with mingled anguish and compassion, but he didn't read it that way at all. He cursed under his breath and rode quickly ahead of her, leaving her to follow behind him with her heart in her shoes. She knew then that he was never going to give in. He wouldn't marry again, because the specter of not having children was too much for him to bear. He'd never be convinced that she could be happy without them, so no matter what his feelings for her were, marriage was out of the question. He'd made that clear just now, without saying a single word.

She was sore and shaky when they got back to the barn. Dane saw her grimace and reached up to help her down. But, as always, the feel of her body triggered helpless longings in his own.

He let her slide down against him, his hands firm on her waist, his eyes holding hers.

"I like your friends," she whispered huskily.

"So do I." He had to fight to breathe normally. He looked down at her soft mouth and all but groaned. "We have to go back."

She drew in an unsteady breath. "I enjoyed the ride."

"Sore?"

She nodded and smiled. "I'm not used to horses, but I think I could learn to like riding."

He searched her eyes slowly. "I could learn to like a lot of things, if I let myself." His face hardened. "I want you so," he whispered roughly. "But I can't have you."

"Dane..."

He let go of her and moved back. "No. In a day or two, we'll wrap up your problem. Then we'll get on with our lives."

He turned to lead the horses into the barn. He had shut her out. Just that easily, he turned his back on what had happened, on any future that contained both of them. As they drove back to Houston, Tess thought she'd never felt quite so alone.

As long as she and Dane were communicating, she'd been able to push what had happened with the attempted kidnapping to the back of her mind. That, and the trap they were going to set the following Monday night for the men. Now she worried over it until her hands were twisting nervously in her lap. If anything went wrong, she could die this time. She glanced at Dane and wondered if losing her would hurt him at all. That was unfair, she thought. Of course he'd care if she died. He was a caring man, despite his misgivings about her role in his life.

He saw her worried face. "What's wrong?" he asked quietly.

"I was thinking about the trap," she said, surprising him. He hadn't let himself consider the upcoming event, because it disturbed him so much. Now he was forced to think about it, and to worry about what might happen if something went wrong.

His chest rose and fell heavily. "Try to remember that Nick and I are fairly competent at what we do for a living," he said after a minute, his voice deep and slow. "We'll take good care of you, little one. We'll get them."

She smiled wanly. "Okay."

She didn't sound convinced, but he couldn't dwell on that. He had to hope that the scenario would play as he and Nick had rehearsed it. Once the assailants were in custody, he could decide what to do about Tess. One thing was certain. He had to get her out of his life before he weakened and let her stay. For her own sake, that couldn't happen. He cared too much to let her settle for a barren marriage, even if it was going to kill him to let her go.

Seven

The darkness outside the windows was dismal. Rain had begun to pepper down. It was a cold rain. Tess wrapped her arms around her body, because even the gray sweater she was wearing over dark slacks and a blue-and-gray-patterned blouse didn't spare her from the chill. Behind her, Dane was smoking a cigarette, waiting.

Out of sight were Nick and Helen and Adams, along with two of Sergeant Graves's best men. Some subtle investigative work had revealed that the office was being watched. Tonight, the office staff was going to take advantage of that surveillance to spring a trap. Dane and Tess were apparently working late. The rest of the office staff had left earlier, with a great deal of noise, so that anyone watching would see them. Once out of sight, they'd parked their cars several blocks away and had crept back into position, as planned.

Dane checked his watch. He was uneasy. He hadn't wanted to do this, but he had no choice. He couldn't let it drag on, let Tess be constantly in danger. He might not be quick enough the next time. The drug lords had already gotten to her. At least this way, he had a good chance of success in catching them once and for all.

He didn't want her threatened. He couldn't keep her, but he couldn't bear to see her hurt, ever.

"Scared?" he asked gently.

"Terrified," she confessed. "That's normal, isn't it?" she added, turning. "It isn't lack of fear that creates heroes. It's going ahead, doing what you have to when you're so frightened you can hardly stand on your feet."

He nodded. "That's it, exactly. I've been in gun battles more than once. Every time, I could taste the fear. But I never ran."

She smiled. "The adrenaline surge you get from danger is powerful," she remarked. "Once I was away from the drug people and running, I could have flown."

He scowled. "It's addictive," he said quietly. "That's why I'd never let you work as an operative. You'd have taken to the danger without hesitation. It would have put you at risk constantly."

"You're at risk constantly," she pointed out. Her eyes slid over his hard, lean face. "But you won't quit, either."

"I don't have anyone to leave behind," he said. His expression dared her to argue. "This isn't a married man's— or woman's—occupation, not the way we operate. The demands of the job can kill the best of relationships. Jane hated my work when I was a ranger. I was never home."

Her eyes softened. "Dane, if you'd loved her, really loved her . . . wouldn't you have been?"

His face went expressionless. He turned his wrist and glanced at his watch. "It's time." He put out his cigarette.

She asked questions he didn't want to answer. "You know what to do."

"Yes."

He picked up his attaché case, hesitating as he passed her. His dark eyes caressed her face. "Don't take chances. If it goes down unexpectedly, scream, break a window, do anything to get my attention. I won't be out of earshot, no matter what."

"All right." She swallowed. Her mouth was dry, her palms sweaty. Her heartbeat was racing, but she couldn't let him see how frightened she was. It would only make things worse.

"You've got plenty of backup," he added. "It's going to be all right. After tonight, it will be over."

"They can make bail again...."

"Not in this case. If it's permitted, we'll make sure it's set high enough that they'll never raise it."

"It's still my word against theirs."

"After tonight it won't be," he promised. He touched her lips with his forefinger. "Chin up, lover," he breathed. He bent his head and nipped her lower lip hard, making her mouth open so that he could take it hungrily. But before she could reach up to hold him, he was out the door.

She was alone. The office was suddenly cold and frightening. She paced nervously. Dane had had time to get to the parking lot, get to his car and put the attaché case in the trunk. From there, he was going to light a cigarette and then start back toward the office. It would look as if he'd just stepped out for a minute, not as if he was deliberately leaving Tess alone—that would have been a dead giveaway to anyone watching that it was a setup.

In those few minutes, a dark brown sedan had purred to a stop down the street and two men had emerged. From the shadows, they'd eased along the side of the building, keeping Dane in sight until he rounded the corner at the parking lot.

They'd seen their opportunity and they took it. Darting into the building and then into the elevator, they went up to the floor where the office was located. When the elevator stopped, they were already drawing their weapons. This time they were taking no chances. None at all.

What they didn't know was that Dane had seen them. Wasting no time, he'd darted around to the back of the building and the service elevator. There was a back way into his office. He had his .45 automatic out, cocked, and in his hand when the main door to the office began to open. Tess had turned automatically to look when she heard the sound. The flash of the first man's gun burned into her consciousness, leaving her rigid, unable to move. She wasn't going to make it. She knew that no operative was going to have time to get to her before the shots hit her. Remembering the pain she'd known before, she stared at the pistol with blank, terror-filled eyes. *Dane,* she thought in anguish. Her last conscious thought was of him.

"Duck!"

The voice commanded and she obeyed, falling to the floor even as the sound of automatic gunfire shattered the silence.

Dane hit the floor near her, rolling to escape the bullets with all his ex-policeman's skill. He had only one instant to aim and fire, but he was an expert shot. He had one clear shot at the first man with the small Uzi in his hands, and he took it. The drug dealer's gun discharged again and suddenly flew out of his hands seconds before he caught his shoulder and went down, crying out as the bullet hit him. The second man whirled and ran. Dane leaped to his feet with fluid grace, his face set in lines Tess had never seen, his eyes black fires in a stony countenance as he spun the wounded man onto his belly and searched him with quick deft motions. He always carried handcuffs. He snapped them onto the man's wrists and left him, coming back to Tess, who was by now on her knees and shaking from the experience.

"The other man," she gasped.

He took her arm and pulled her to her feet. "Nick will have him by now."

"Get me a doctor, damn you!" the downed man cried. "This is inhuman! I'm bleeding!"

"So was Tess when you shot her," he replied, adding a few adjectives that turned Tess's face ruddy.

"Are you all right?" she asked Dane, her hands unconsciously searching his arms for wounds. "He didn't hit you?"

A corner of his mouth tugged up. "I've spent most of my life dodging bullets," he reminded her. "I used to get paid for it. Are you all right?"

"I am now," she said, and leaned against him weakly, her cheek on his chest. She stared at the downed man, who was curled up, groaning. Blood stained his elegant jacket. The Uzi he'd brought with him was dangling from one of Dane's lean hands.

"Tess!"

Helen's voice echoed loudly as she leaped from the elevator with Nick right behind. "We heard shots..." She stopped, staring at the downed man briefly before she studied Dane and Tess. "Everybody okay?"

"We're fine. How about his cohort?" Dane asked, nodding toward the wounded man.

"I handed him over to Sergeant Graves's men," Nick said, reholstering his automatic. He gave Helen a dark glare from eyes almost as black as Dane's. "No thanks to my sister, Miss James Bond, here," he added. "She actually walked into the line of fire."

"I did not!" Helen raged. "You came out of nowhere Why is it always my fault anytime something goes wrong?" she demanded. "Don't you ever make mistakes, Mr. Perfect?"

"No," he said with a pleasant smile.

Dane had to stifle a grin at the expression on Helen's face "Cut it out," he said. "Call an ambulance for our victim there," he instructed, handing Helen the Uzi.

"Careful, don't get fingerprints on it," Nick said with deliberate sarcasm.

"I know how to hold a gun," she said smugly. "You taught me yourself! Are you okay?" she asked Tess.

"I'm fine, thanks," Tess said breathlessly.

"Damned detectives," the downed man spat. "Damned detectives!"

Dane lifted an eyebrow and drew Tess closer. "Come on," he said gently. "Let's get you out of here."

It was a long night. She had to give a statement, wait until it was typed and read back to her, then sign it. The wounded man was taken to the hospital under police guard Later he'd be removed to the county jail pending trial. The other man was booked and jailed and his lawyer was telephoned.

No bail, Dane had promised. Tess breathed easily for the first time.

She slept without being coaxed, right past the alarm clock. When she woke, there was a note from Dane, telling her not to come to work that day, that she needed the rest

Probably she did. And she needed the time to pack, she thought miserably. He hadn't said so, but then he'd barely spoken to her the night before. He'd been kind but impersonal, and he hadn't offered more than cursory comfort He'd sent her to bed, insisting that she needed sleep more than conversation.

But what he really wanted was to see the last of her. She didn't need a crystal ball to understand that he wasn't going to let her into his life on any permanent basis. Probably, now that she was out of danger, he wasn't even going to want her in the office anymore. Her very presence would be a painful reminder of his vulnerability, of the night he'd given in to his need of her and let himself love her.

He *did* love her. That was the only certainty she had. But he was going to fight it, and he might win. That was the chance she was taking by complying with his wishes; by going away without argument. She had to draw back and let him think it out for himself. Only by giving him freedom of choice did she have any chance of convincing him that they could have a future together.

She packed her things and had them ready when he came home that evening. She was sitting on the sofa, dressed in neat gray slacks with a white bulky-knit sweater, her hair in a braid down her back, her coat next to her.

She looked up as he entered the apartment. He paused at the sight of her suitcases, scowling.

"I thought you'd prefer it like this," she said quietly. "No fuss. No trouble." She stood up. "Can you drive me home, please?"

He drew in a slow breath. She was right. It was better this way. But he'd expected to find her curled up on the sofa, as she'd been so many evenings, watching television. The stark reality of her departure hit him like a body blow.

"Come on," he said, his voice as stiff as his posture. "I'll do that before I get comfortable."

"Thank you."

She put on her coat and followed him out of the apartment. She didn't look back. It would have broken her heart.

"You don't have to worry about your assailants," he told her. "I have assurances that they won't get out again. You'll have to testify. Graves will notify you."

"So he said." She concentrated on the streetlights and didn't speak again. She was too choked up for that.

When they arrived at her apartment, it was cold. She turned up the thermostat while Dane unloaded her suitcases and brought them in. He stood there, elegant in a vested navy blue suit, his posture arrow-straight.

"Will you be okay?" he asked.

"Of course. I'm safe, now—right?" she added nervously. "They don't have friends who owe them favors, or anything?"

He shook his head. "Fortunately, these two are jumpups—renegades who poached on another pusher's territory. Nobody loves them enough to make you pay for their arrest."

"Thank God."

He studied her quietly, with faint sadness in his expression, in his eyes. "You don't have to come in tomorrow if you don't feel like it."

"I won't mind getting back to work." She wrapped her arms around herself and looked up. "If you won't mind letting me stay... ?"

"My God, that would be gratitude, wouldn't it?" he asked harshly. "Turning you out on the streets when you took a bullet on my account!"

"It wasn't on your account. I saw something I shouldn't have. I never blamed you."

He drew in a rough breath. "Well, I do. I blame myself for a hell of a lot of things."

"I'm a big girl now," she told him bravely. "I made my own choices, Dane."

"Did you?" he asked, his dark eyes narrowing as they searched hers. He watched her blush. "Maybe you think you had a choice. I'm not sure you really did. I seduced you."

She smiled sadly and shook her head. "I'm afraid it was the other way around."

He lit a cigarette, his shoulders slumping a little as he smoked it, watching her quietly. "You'll get over this," he said, searching her sad eyes. "You don't think so, but you will. God knows, people can get over any kind of pain eventually."

"Jane hurt you badly, didn't she?" she asked. "I wouldn't, but you can't be sure of that, because you don't trust emotions. Do you really want to be alone for the rest of your life, Dane?"

"Yes," he said curtly. He averted his eyes so that she wouldn't see the lie in them. He wanted Tess, but getting out of her life was the kindest thing he could do for her. When she was happily married, with children, she'd forget him.

Tess didn't know how to answer the stark statement he'd just made. She couldn't convince him. Words wouldn't be enough. Her body wasn't enough to tempt him to stay with her. She had nothing left, except the fact that she loved him, and he didn't believe that. With one word, he'd robbed her of every convincing argument she had.

"Then there's nothing left to say."

"Nothing," he agreed. His eyes searched around the small apartment and then went back to her, lingering only for an instant. He turned then, and opened the door. "I'll see you in the morning."

"In the morning," she whispered, fighting tears.

His back stiffened as he heard her choked tone. He didn't look at her. It would have been fatal. "Take care of yourself."

"I'll do that. You, too." She hesitated. "Dane?"

"What?"

"Thank you for saving my life. If you hadn't been in the office, I wouldn't be here now."

His eyes closed. A wave of nausea washed over him. He couldn't think about that. He couldn't bear the pain of remembering how close she'd come to death, twice now. "Good night, Tess," he said tightly. He went out and closed the door, only then lifting his hot face to the cold night air, swallowing down the sick lump in his throat.

There was rain, and more rain. He walked back to the car, but he didn't get into it. He turned and leaned against it, his eyes on the lighted windows of Tess's apartment complex. He was always on the outside looking in, he thought bitterly, always standing in the cold rain and looking at warm windows. If he could have given Tess a child, he might have been inside even now, holding her, loving her. But he couldn't give her that, and he'd be cheating her if he gave in to his own feelings.

He finished his cigarette and threw it to the pavement, watching it fizzle out in the puddle of rain. He felt like that, as if a fire inside him had been coldly quenched. He turned and got into the car and drove away into the night.

When they were back at work again, Tess expected coldness from Dane. What she hadn't expected was total indifference. Dane treated her like he did the computer. He extracted information from her, replaced it with other information, and left her sitting in the office without a backward glance when he went home. It was boss-employee now, all the way.

She went through the motions of working, but her heart wasn't in it. Dane didn't want her around. She knew he hated even the sight of her at her desk, but she couldn't make herself do what he really wanted her to. She couldn't resign.

"Want to go out and have a pizza with me?" Helen offered, grinning. "Now that I'm a heroine, with my name in the papers," she added, because the arrest had made headlines, "the pizza-parlor owner thinks I'm the berries. He gives me anything I want." She snapped her fingers. "Even double cheese and mushrooms and anchovies."

"You'll start melting one day," Tess cautioned. "All that pizza will turn your poor insides into mozzarella and you'll ooze all over the floor."

"Not as long as I eat enough anchovies to keep me solvent." The older woman grinned. "Come on. Come home with me. You look dismal these days, all pale and worn. You need cheering up."

"I don't feel like going out," Tess said. "I get sleepy with the chickens these days. Residue from all the pressure," she added with a smile. "I still have to go to court next month when the trial comes up." Her assailants had since been arraigned and a trial date had been set.

"The vultures," Helen muttered. "I hope they get life."

"Unlikely," Tess replied. "But they'll very probably spend some time in jail. I hope I'm living in Antarctica when they get out," she added, shivering.

"Haven't you heard?" Helen asked. "I thought Dane would have told you that they've been implicated in the murder of a rival drug lord. He was shot with an Uzi, and ballistics matched the fatal bullet to the Uzi that wild man was shooting in here the night we apprehended them. It isn't you they'll be doing time for assaulting—the DA's going for murder one and two counts of possession with intent to distribute. He figures that's more than enough, even without your assault charge, although they may use it if they think they need to."

"Dane didn't mention that." Tess didn't add that Dane only spoke to her when it was absolutely necessary, or that he avoided her like the plague most of the time.

Helen's eyes narrowed. "He doesn't look much better than you do," she remarked. "Poor guy, he lost a lot of sleep while you were in danger. I don't suppose he's caught up yet, and he's taken on a double caseload since the arrest. I suppose he's trying to use up some of that nervous energy."

"I suppose so." Tess yawned. "I wish I had some of it. I'm so tired!"

"Maybe you do need an early night at that. Come have a pizza with me. It'll cheer you up, and I'll get you home so you can catch up on your beauty sleep."

"Thanks, but really, I don't want anything spicy, anyway. My stomach's been queasy for a couple of days. I'm afraid it's that stomach bug Adams had. He breathed on me."

"Harold's got a cold. I'll bring him to the office and have him breathe on Adams for you," Helen offered.

"You're a real friend," Tess said fervently.

Helen grinned. "Don't I know it."

After work, Tess went home and went to bed. The virus was potent, she thought as she lost her breakfast the next morning. She called in sick and curled up in bed again, listening to the pouring rain outside with vague pleasure as she went back to sleep.

Dane came by after work to check on her. She was astonished that he bothered. His attitude in the office had convinced her that he'd put her completely out of his mind.

"How are you?" he asked at the doorway.

She was disheveled and pale, clad in a worn cotton gown and a thick, red chenille bathrobe that covered her from head almost to bare toes. "I've just got Adams's virus," she said weakly. "Shoot him for me, will you?"

"Can I get you anything?"

She shook her head. "Thanks, but I've got frozen yogurt. It's keeping me alive."

He hesitated. "Maybe you should see a doctor," he said with a frown.

"For a stomach bug? Sure." She held the door open pointedly. "I need to lie down, Dane. Thanks for coming by, but I'll be okay in a couple of days. You can get a temp while I'm out, can't you?"

"We had one today." He hesitated. "She's very good. Her dictation skills and typing speeds are on par with yours."

"If you want me to resign, you only have to say so," she told him softly, her eyes meeting his. She caught a look on his face that confirmed her suspicions. "Talk to her and see if she'll agree to stay," she told him. "If she will, and you'll let me go without proper notice..."

"You can't leave until you've got another job to go to," he said through his teeth.

"Short Investigations will hire me in a minute. You know that. Mr. Short said once when he was collaborating with you on a case that he'd love to have me work for him."

Mr. Short was in his forties and good-looking, a widower with style and daring. Dane's eyes narrowed as he thought about Tess in the same office with that man.

"I don't think so...." he began.

"Dane, you don't want me around," she said wearily. "Let's stop pretending. Since you slept with me, I'm a perpetual thorn in your side. You look at me like you can't stand the sight of me. I understand. It's just as hard for me to work with you, knowing you feel that way. Let me go. I'll be all right."

He winced. "Don't look like that," he said huskily. "You make me feel two inches tall."

"I don't mean to." She leaned against the wall beside the door, her eyes loving him unconsciously. "Maybe I can forget, if I don't have to see you everyday," she said weakly.

"You'll find someone else," he said through his teeth.

"I know," she said to placate his conscience. Not that she believed it. Love like hers didn't wear out. She forced a smile for him. "Goodbye, Dane."

"It couldn't work, honey," he said, his voice so tender and anguished that she could have cried. "We'd have two strikes against us from the beginning. I don't want marriage."

"I know," she said softly. "It's all right."

His chest rose and fell heavily. "No, it's not. I miss you. I'm alone. Nothing is the same anymore."

Tears filled her eyes, threatening to spill over. "Please go, before I make an even bigger fool of myself," she pleaded.

"It isn't love you feel for me!" he ground out. "Don't you see? It's just physical!"

She couldn't answer him. Her eyes, in her thin, pale face, were tragic.

"It's for the best. You'll realize it eventually. You'll marry and have a houseful of kids...." He turned away before his voice broke. He couldn't bear to think about that. "Goodbye, little one. I'll have Helen bring by your severance pay. You can tell her you can't bear the memories of the shooting. She'll believe it."

"I'll do that," she choked. *Please leave,* she was thinking frantically, *please leave before I break down and go to pieces!*

His shoulders squared. "If you ever need me..."

"Thank you. Good night."

He didn't look back. He started to, but his control was precarious.

He went out and heard the door close behind him. It broke his heart to walk away and leave Tess, but he had nothing to give her. She didn't really love him, he told himself. It was just physical attraction. And marriage was impossible and unfair to Tess. He kept telling himself that all the way home.

But when he was back in his empty apartment, the only thing that registered was that he was totally alone.

Eight

Mr. Short did indeed want Tess to work for him. The following Monday, when she was feeling a little better, she went in for an interview.

The tall, distinguished man had an office full of people, just like Dane. This office was less rigid, though, and Desden Short's operatives were a little more haphazard than Tess liked. The position he was offering her was that of skip tracer, not secretary, and she was delighted.

"I never expected . . . !" she exclaimed.

"I haven't forgotten how you moaned about being only a secretary at Lassister's agency," he chuckled. "Skip tracing isn't as dangerous and demanding as being a full-fledged operative, but it might satisfy your thirst for stealth and excitement. We'll see."

"I can't thank you enough!"

"Yes, you can. Work hard and make me proud." He stood up and shook hands with her. "If you can stay today,

Mary can explain the job to you and help you get accli-
mated. She doesn't leave until next Monday, so that gives
you a week to familiarize yourself with the operation before you have to start work.''

"Fine," she agreed, smiling. "I'll enjoy it, I know I will.
I'll work hard."

"What puzzles me is why Dane let you go," he said with
a curious smile. "You were practically related."

"It was the shooting," she lied. "The office has such bad
memories for me now that I get cold chills just sitting in it."

His curiosity faded. "I see." He smiled. "Well, we'll do
our best not to let you get shot here."

"Thanks," she murmured dryly.

Mary Plummer was thirty, a blonde like Tess, and viva-
cious. "You're going to love this," she said, introducing
Tess to the tools of the trade. "It's a plum job, and I'll even
give you the names of all my contacts at the public agencies. You can pump them for information when you're really stuck. This," she said, picking up a thick book, "is
something you've probably seen plenty of times at Lassiter's.''

"Yes," Tess agreed. "It's Cole's—the directory that gives
names and addresses for telephone numbers. Dane said once
that no detective agency could operate without one."

"Amen. It's the most important book I own. Here. It's
yours now. Take good care of it, and it will take good care
of you."

"You're a real friend."

"That's what my fiancé says. We're getting married Saturday, and by Monday, I hope to be sailing in the Bahamas, never to return. He's filthy rich." She sighed. "But I'd
love him if he were a pauper."

Tess knew how that felt. Not a day went by that she didn't
think of Dane and wish she could be back with him again.
That might never happen. She'd resigned herself to the fact

that it was highly unlikely he'd willingly come after her now. He'd convinced himself that she was only infatuated with him and that she wanted things he could never give her. She'd been so certain that he loved her, but as time passed without even a word from him, she grew depressed and unsure of herself.

"You look very pale," Mary observed. "Are you sure you're over that virus?"

"Of course I am," Tess replied.

But weeks went by and she didn't get appreciably better. If anything, her stomach problems grew worse. She convinced herself that it was an ulcer. With all the pressure she'd been under—being shot, being stalked, losing Dane, changing jobs—no wonder she was having problems.

She settled into her new job, though, determined not to let her bad health get her down.

Helen insisted on meeting her for lunch a month after she'd left the agency. She'd tried before and Tess had refused, but this time Helen wouldn't be put off, so Tess gave in.

"You really do look bad," Helen said without preamble, frowning as they sat eating cheddar-cheese soup in a sandwich shop.

"It's all the pressure, I think," Tess told her. "So many changes in so little time."

"You've lost weight. You're pale."

"Nerves. Mr. Short is a great boss, but I'm doing a job I've never tried before."

"I suppose so." Helen wasn't convinced. She watched the younger girl with narrowed eyes. "Dane is—"

"How about some ice cream for dessert?" Tess changed the subject, forcing a smile.

Helen didn't speak for an instant. But she got the message. She smiled. "Okay. Point taken. Ice cream it is."

Tess enjoyed the meal after that, but she didn't enjoy the memories it brought back. She'd actually kept Dane out of her mind for a whole day just recently, until Helen came along and opened the floodgates.

Tess went back to her apartment that night and cried herself to sleep. She was so hungry for Dane that even the sound of his name on someone else's lips made her heart beat faster. She'd told herself that she could live without him, but doing it was proving impossible. She couldn't go on like this. She couldn't bear it!

The next morning, she got up and started to leave the apartment, and fainted dead away.

When she came to, it dawned on her that something was very wrong with her. It had been weeks since she'd left the agency, six since she'd left Dane's apartment. That was over a month with the strange virus that had assailed her, ruined her appetite, made her tired. She had all the symptoms of cancer, she told herself, and it was stupid not to see a doctor. Having only an ulcer would be a blessing. Being scared to death was no excuse for hiding her head in the sand. Knowing the truth was always best.

She called for an appointment, and got in that very morning for an examination with the local family practitioner she'd been going to. They must have thought she was terminal, she thought with bitter humor as she phoned the office to tell them she was going to be late.

It was a routine examination until she explained her symptoms to Dr. Reiner. He sat down on his stool and stared at her.

"I have to ask you something you aren't going to like," he began quietly. "Have you been intimate with a man in the past several weeks?"

Her heart jumped wildly. "Yes," she blurted out. "Once. Well, one night..."

"That would do it," he said on a sigh.

"But he's . . . sterile," she faltered. "He said . . . that he couldn't father a child."

He cocked an eyebrow. "When was your last period?"

She thought back; she hadn't realized that she'd missed one. She swallowed and told him her best guess.

"We'll run tests," he said. "I'm sorry, Miss Meriwether, but I think you're pregnant. The symptoms certainly fit."

It was like a blow to the solar plexus. She touched her stomach with wonder, her eyes wide and wild-looking.

"It isn't the end of the world," he said quietly. "There's a clinic nearby . . ."

"No!" She paled, gasping, her hand flattening protectively over the child she might be carrying. "Oh, no, not ever!"

"You want it, then?"

"With all my heart," she whispered. "I've never wanted anything in my life as much!"

"And the father?"

"I'm afraid he probably won't believe it's his," she said sadly. "In any case, he doesn't believe in marriage, so it's not something I need to bother him with. Not now. When I'm sure . . . I'll make the decision then."

"Very well. I'll send Nurse Wallace in and we'll get started." He patted her shoulder absently. "Don't worry about it."

Not easy to do, she thought. She couldn't help worrying. The thought of being responsible for a tiny human being was almost as terrifying as a fatal illness. She'd get over it, though, she told herself. People had been having babies for thousands of years. Presumably every mother was afraid of the responsibility at first.

They ran tests and Tess spent a long, sleepless night worrying about it. She hadn't told anyone at the office what the doctor suspected. But when she answered the phone at work, and she heard the nurse's calm voice telling her that she was, indeed, pregnant, she had to struggle to not fall over. She numbly thanked the woman and hung up, without waiting to schedule her next appointment or talk about referral to an obstetrician. That, she decided vaguely, could wait one more day.

"You've gone white," Delcy, the other skip tracer, said worriedly. "Tess, are you all right?"

"All right." Tess nodded.

"Want some coffee?"

"No. Yes. I don't know. Thank you."

Delcy began to laugh. "What *was* that phone call? A proposal from a boyfriend?"

Tess fought to pull herself together. "Sorry," she said, flushing. "No, it was the doctor's office telling me that I'm going to be all right."

"Thank goodness. You've had us all worried."

"Me, too," Tess confessed. She sat back in the chair, her hand resting protectively on her stomach. She was carrying Dane's child. He wouldn't know. He probably wouldn't even believe it was his. But she knew, and the thought of having a child was suddenly magical, awesome.

For the rest of the day, Tess did her job mechanically. A big part of a detective agency's routine was finding missing people: deserting spouses, runaway teens, felons skipping out on bail, people trying to outrun debtors, even adopted children trying to find natural parents for one reason or another. Usually, a good skip tracer could find a missing person in under an hour, with some help from contacts at public agencies and a little careful conversation. It wasn't exactly deductive reasoning on the order of Sherlock Holmes's, but it served a purpose and it could be rewarding. The day before, when she'd gone to work after visiting the doctor, Tess had located a runaway teenage boy who was trying to make enough money to go home to his frantic parents. The ensuing reunion had earned Tess a tearful phone call of gratitude from parents and son. She'd gone home feeling a little less brittle than usual, feeling useful again.

Today was less successful, probably because she was preoccupied. She succeeded in locating a man whose wife was tracking him down to recover a year's worth of child-support payments. She was glad the man didn't know who at the agency had found him, but all the same Mr. Short was on the receiving end of some nasty language and a veiled threat.

"I'm really sorry...." Tess began when he hung up.

He laughed with real delight. "Tess, it goes with the job," he said. "I'll bet Dane got his ears burned every day. People in trouble don't like being found. That's human nature."

Mention of Dane made her uncomfortable. She nodded.

"You're just nervous because of what happened to you," he guessed. "That was a once-in-a-lifetime thing, having a felon try to hurt you. You'll never be in the line of fire here, okay?"

"Okay."

He paused by her desk, his eyes narrow and speculative. "I don't usually mix business with pleasure, but how would you like to have dinner with me tonight?"

She was shocked by the suggestion. Dane was in her past now and she was pregnant, but it was as if she'd been asked to commit adultery just by going out with a man.

"Thank you very much," she said genuinely. "but I can't, if you don't mind. I'm ... getting over someone."

"Ah. I see." He smiled. "Time does heal wounds, you know. I'll ask again, one of these days."

She nodded, but she didn't encourage him. She had enough upheaval in her life at the moment.

* * *

Houston was a big city, and because she was confined to the office, she didn't see much of it. That was good. There was very little chance of running into Dane. But as a month became two, and then three, Kit came home. And life became tedious.

Tess wanted so badly to call Dane and tell him about the baby. But he'd said, over and over, that he didn't want to marry again, that he didn't want commitment. She couldn't tell him she was pregnant because he'd feel obliged to marry her. Even if he wanted the child, how could she put him in such a position? And what if, heaven forbid, he didn't believe it was his? He'd told her he was sterile. He might accuse her of being with another man.

There was, as well, one really good reason why she shouldn't say anything just yet. She was having some pain and a good deal of spotting. She knew those were bad symptoms, and so did her doctor, who promptly made an appointment for her with the obstetrician when she described them to him. She had to find out exactly what was wrong. If she was in danger of losing the child, telling Dane would be the worst thing she could do.

In the end, her muddled mind simply avoided thinking about the problem. But it didn't go away.

"*Why* can't you come and have lunch with me today?" Kit moaned. "I'm just home from Italy! Mr. Deverell is giving me fits! I want to assassinate him. I've got to talk to you!"

She couldn't go have lunch with Kit because Kit worked just down the street from the Lassiter Agency, and the restaurant where she ate was one that Dane frequented. But she couldn't tell Kit that.

"You could drive over here...."

"I don't understand any of this," Kit said heavily. "If it wasn't for Helen, I wouldn't even have known how to get in touch with you. I come home from one little trip and you've changed jobs and moved across town."

"It was necessary."

"This isn't like you, to desert your friends," Kit muttered. "It's something more, I know it is."

"Look, you could come over tonight and I'll tell you all about it."

"Lunch would be quicker."

There was a long pause. Tess tangled the telephone cord in her hands, wary of being overheard. "I can't have lunch at the restaurant. I don't want . . . to run into Dane."

There was a longer pause on the other end. "I had a feeling that might be the case. There's a restaurant that specializes in fish between your office and mine—know where it is?"

"Yes."

"I'll meet you there at noon. Fair enough? Neutral ground?"

"Fair enough."

The restaurant Kit had chosen was busy, but big enough to serve a large lunch crowd. Even though it was miles from Dane's office, Tess's gray eyes slid around nervously until she saw tall, elegant Kit walking toward her. Kit had thick dark hair that curved toward her pixie face, with sparkling blue eyes under long, silky lashes. Tess was tall, but Kit was taller, and thinner at the moment.

The older girl stared at Tess and frowned. "You've gained weight, haven't you?" she asked, indicating the loose, white knit sweater Tess was wearing. Her charcoal slacks were two sizes larger than she normally wore, to accommodate her expanding waistline. Her face was fuller, too; more radiant.

"I've gained a little," Tess confessed. "There's an Italian restaurant near the agency."

"I hear you're working as a skip tracer now," Kit said, shaking her head. "It took you long enough to decide to fight Dane's influence. He'd never have let you do anything like that while you worked for him. He's hopelessly overprotective."

Tess was stiff, unusually so, as they were seated and given menus.

Kit stared at her intently. "You might as well tell me. I'm not going to give up until you do."

"I'm pregnant," Tess blurted out, her lips trembling.

Kit became statue-still, as if she'd stopped breathing. "Dane's?" she asked finally, letting out a slow breath.

"Yes."

The older girl began to smile, her eyes quietly compassionate. "And he doesn't know," she said.

Tess nodded, dropping her eyes to the menu. She could hardly see it for the mist in front of her.

"His marriage failed," Kit said gently. "He's running scared. Everybody knows. Not only that, he lost the job he loved, along with his mother, and he's not as able physically as he used to be. It's natural that he'd fight getting involved again, especially with someone as vulnerable as you." She touched Tess's cold hand. "You're going to tell him, aren't you, eventually?"

"Eventually. Not now."

"Why?"

Tess hesitated. "I've been having some problems. I've got an appointment to see my obstetrician tomorrow morning." She grimaced. "His nurse didn't sound very encouraging when I gave her my symptoms." She looked up worriedly. "I've got one of those all-purpose medical books. It could be early signs of a miscarriage," she said nervously. "Kit, what will I do? I can't lose it now, I just can't! It's all I've got . . . !"

Kit clasped the cold fingers firmly. "Get hold of yourself," she said, her voice reassuring. "It's all right, Tess. It's all right. Take a deep breath. And another. That's it. Listen to me—you've got to stop this. Don't start thinking negatively. It's dangerous."

"But what will I do—" She stopped in midsentence and her face became drained of color as she saw who was coming in the door.

"Dane," Kit guessed before she turned around. She winced. "He never comes here!"

Not only was he there, his eyes were searching the restaurant as if he were looking for someone. When his gaze found Tess, he started visibly. His face tautened and he made a beeline for her.

"No," Tess whispered huskily. "He can't . . . !"

But he did. He paused by the table, his dark eyes sliding with quiet desperation over Tess's wan face, as if he couldn't get enough of just looking at her. "We haven't seen you in weeks," he said curtly. "I thought you might at least stop by once in a while to say hello. Or don't you care enough?"

That was a strange question from someone who'd as much as admitted that he couldn't bear the sight of her.

"I work across town," she said, schooling her voice to remain calm even though she was shaking inside. "It's difficult for me to get away."

"Yes. I understand that you're doing a skip tracer's job now."

She lifted her chin. "Yes. It's nice to do a little real detective work for a change."

He searched her gray eyes slowly, and she saw shadows in his that she couldn't define. She couldn't know he'd been starving for her. The apartment was empty, his job was empty, his life was empty. He'd never thought he was capable of missing someone so much. The fact that she'd gone away and stayed away made him vicious. She'd sworn undying love, but she didn't seem to be dying without him. She couldn't be bothered to phone the office or visit, not even to see Helen or have lunch with her friend Kit.

"Detective work is dangerous," he said shortly.

"Yes, I know. I got shot, didn't I?"

He drew in a slow breath, ramming his lean hands into the pockets of his gray slacks. He looked worn. "You might at least call us once in a while, so we know you're still alive."

"I'll try to do that," Tess replied. She averted her eyes to the table. "I suppose Helen does miss me."

His jaw clenched. His hands curled into fists. Yes, Helen missed her. But not like he did. He wanted to tell her how much, but she acted as if she wouldn't have believed him. Her whole attitude was one of indifference. *How, Tess?* he thought bitterly. *How can you be like this, after what we shared that night?*

It didn't help him to remember that her departure had been his idea. He hadn't wanted commitment, he'd told her. But that was before he'd tried to face life without her beside him. He hated going home at night, because Tess wouldn't be in the apartment when he got there. He hated his very life, empty and cold and unsatisfying because she was no longer part of it. His dark eyes caressed her bent head and he sighed. He'd sent her away. Now he couldn't get her back. He didn't know what to do. Had he killed every shred of feeling she'd had for him?

"Don't you want to join us, Dane?" Kit asked when the silence grew tense and prolonged.

"No," he said absently. "I have to get back to work. Tess?"

She looked up, wounded by the false tenderness in his deep drawl. "Yes?"

He searched her drawn face quietly. "Are you all right?" he asked gently. "You look..." He wasn't sure how she looked. Sick. Worried. "Have you been ill again?"

The color surged back into her cheeks. She averted her face. "Winter brings on plenty of colds, you know," she replied evasively. It hurt her to look at him. She didn't dare do it for long, or everything she felt would rush into her eyes and betray her. She was carrying his child under her heart, and she couldn't tell him. It hurt . . . !

She gasped as a stab of pain went through her. It was a familiar pain—one she had every time she did a lot of walking just lately—and the reason she'd called the obstetrician's office for an appointment.

"Tess!"

Dane was beside her, kneeling, his hand grasping hers, his dark eyes full of concern. "What is it, little one?" he asked quickly. "Are you all right?"

"I think I have an ulcer, that's all," she hedged. The touch of his hand was driving her mad, sending waves of helpless pleasure through her body. She lifted her eyes and met his, and the world stopped. Everything stopped. She looked at him and her heart broke in two inside her body.

His face contorted. His eyes were tormented. "Tess," he groaned, his voice as haunted as his eyes.

She took a slow breath and shivered at the need for him that still consumed her. "I'm okay," she whispered. "Really, Dane."

His hand was clutching hers bruisingly. He realized it and loosened his grip. Neither of them noticed Kit, who was sipping coffee and trying to be invisible.

"See a doctor, will you?" he asked tightly. "Don't take chances with your health."

"I'll do that," she promised. Her eyes slid to his mouth and she forcefully levered them back up to his. "Are *you* all right?" she asked softly.

Her voice made him warm all over. His cheeks went ruddy as he looked at her, and his heart raced. "No," he said huskily. He drew in a sharp breath, fighting down the need to beg her to come back. "Maybe I miss you, pretty girl," he drawled, his smile faintly mocking.

"Maybe beans walk," she returned, smiling back.

His broad shoulders rose and fell. "You could do skip tracing for me, I guess," he murmured reluctantly.

"You've got three skip tracers already," she reminded him, although the offer made her tingle. He had to miss her a little, even if he didn't want to.

"I'll fire one," he offered.

She laughed. "No. I'm happy with Mr. Short, Dane," she said after a minute. "It wouldn't work out."

"You could give it a chance," he said slowly, with an expression in his eyes that she couldn't understand.

"The job?" She faltered.

He hesitated. He wanted to say, *No, not the job, me.* He wanted to ask her to pack a suitcase and move in with him, live with him, sleep with him. Nothing could be as bad as life without her. Perhaps if she cared enough, they could build some kind of marriage even if children were impossible. God knew, he wanted her enough to risk it. She'd loved him once; he knew she had. There might still be time....

But she laughed suddenly again, hiding her own feelings. "I don't want to come back, thanks all the same," she said, sparing him the embarrassment of knowing she was still hopelessly in love with him. She didn't want his pity. "I'm very happy, Dane. I like what I'm doing, and Mr. Short even asked me out. Who knows where it might lead?"

Dane's eyes went black, glittery. "Short's in his forties," he said through his teeth. "Too old and too much of a philanderer...!"

"Is that the time?" Kit interrupted, seeing danger signals ahead. "Gosh, I've got to go, Tess!"

"Yes, I'll be late, too," Tess said, staring pointedly at Dane, who was blocking her exit.

He got to his feet slowly, vibrating with anger. Short, with his Tess! He felt like hitting something.

Tess got to her feet slowly and clasped her bag while Kit left the tip. "It was nice to see you," she said hesitantly.

Dane didn't speak. He looked at her blindly, anger in every line of his tall, fit body. All at once, he frowned. His eyes went over her like hands and the scowl grew worse.

"You've gained weight, haven't you?" he asked suddenly.

"A little." She avoided his piercing gaze. "Too many doughnuts."

"No. No, it suits you," he said hesitantly.

She bit her lower lip almost hard enough to draw blood. She wanted to tell him. It was killing her not to tell him. She had no idea how he'd react, and it would probably be a bad thing, with the problems she'd been having. But it was his right to know. Committed, she raised her eyes to his and opened her mouth to speak. But before she could form a word, a passerby recognized him and stepped forward, hand out, grinning.

"Dane Lassiter! I thought it was you!" the man said enthusiastically.

While Dane was fielding his acquaintance's greeting, Tess darted around him and followed Kit out of the restaurant. It had to be fate, she told herself, her heart racing as she realized how close she'd come to blowing her cover. She shouldn't tell him yet. Not until she'd seen the doctor. After she found out what was wrong, she could make decisions.

"I'll bet he followed me," Kit mused as they went to their respective cars. "He isn't a private detective for nothing. He misses you, Tess. A blind person could see it."

"Missing and loving are two different things," she sighed.

"He had to have cared a little bit. After all, it took two for you to be in that condition," the other girl began.

"I seduced him," Tess said, flushing. "I had some crazy idea that if I could convince him of how deeply I loved him, he might start believing in commitment again. But it didn't work. He couldn't shoot me out of the door fast enough."

"He doesn't look as if he likes having you out the door."

Tess shrugged. "It still isn't enough. I can't go back to work for him. I'd eat my heart out. Especially now, I don't need to be around him. He isn't stupid. Eventually, my condition will become obvious."

"Forgive me, but it's already getting there. He's bound to find out," Kit said.

"I know. I'll deal with that when I have to. Right now, I have to get back to work. Not a word to Helen," she cautioned.

"Not a word to anybody. You know me better than that." Kit frowned. "Tess, I'd do anything I could to help you. I hope you know you can depend on me."

"I do. You're the only friend I have."

"That works both ways. Keep in close touch, okay? And let me know what the doctor says."

"I will." Tess got into her small foreign car and waved as she started it and drove back to work. She felt unnerved, and she wondered if it was only because she'd unexpectedly seen Dane. She was uneasy for the rest of the day, without knowing why.

Nine

Tess was thirty minutes early for her appointment with Dr. Boswick. She hadn't slept or eaten much since the day before. The unexpected pains she'd had in the restaurant had frightened her. Dane had been beside her, holding her hand, and the pain had dissipated much sooner than usual. Mystical, she thought, as if the child had heard its father's voice and had felt compelled to survive. No doctor, she was sure, would subscribe to *that* theory.

Dr. Boswick was right on schedule, so she didn't have to wait long. But the tests he performed told him something she didn't want to hear. He called her into his office and sat down behind his desk, poring through test results, having had her come back after work to talk to him.

He laid down the open file folder and looked at her over his glasses. "How badly do you want this baby?" he asked abruptly. "I know you're single, and not well-to-do, so think carefully before you answer."

She didn't understand what her financial situation had to do with it, but the question was easily answered. "I want him more than anything in the world," she said simply.

He smiled gently. "I'm glad you put it that way, because you've got some hard times ahead and no guarantees even then." He swung forward in the chair and leaned his hands on the desk, aware of her taut, worried expression. "You have a rather rare condition—one we sometimes see in the second or third trimester—where the placenta partially or completely covers the cervix. The placenta stretches, sometimes tears. There can be frequent bleeding and the danger of spontaneous abortion."

"Oh, no!" she ground out.

"It happens to some degree in only about one out of every two hundred pregnancies," he continued. "We found an abnormal placement of the placenta in the ultrasound we did earlier. It usually occurs in women who have had multiple pregnancies, and later than this. You're not that far along. Your case is unusual, but this does happen."

"Is there anything I can do?" she asked frantically. "Anything at all?"

"Yes. You can quit your job and stay home until your pregnancy advances sufficiently that we can ascertain whether or not the placenta is going to detach itself from the cervix. That will probably be until you deliver—a normal delivery, I hope, but sometimes a C-section is mandatory. In the meantime, you won't be able to do a lot of walking, and working at a job isn't advisable, either. For God's sake," he added, "don't take aspirin during your pregnancy."

"I'll remember that." Her face felt tight. She had very little in her savings account. She had monthly bills and she needed the job. But he was telling her that she might sacrifice her child if she didn't stay at home.

"As I said, there are no guarantees. You could still lose the child. There's another reason that you shouldn't be alone. Later on, there's a potential for massive bleeding with this condition. I don't want to frighten you, but you could hemorrhage. If there's any bleeding at all, I want to see you, night or day. That will mean complete bed rest until the bleeding stops. Perhaps hospitalization. You see what I meant when I asked how important this child was to you?"

She nodded, her fingers painfully entwined. "I live alone."

"There's no chance that the father might become involved in the pregnancy?"

She hesitated. Then she shook her head. "He doesn't know."

"He should be told."

"Yes, sir." She wasn't going to tell Dane, but it was easier to agree with the doctor than to argue.

"Good girl. You're going to need help. This won't be easy. Meanwhile, I'll have Bertha set up another appointment. You'll need to come fairly regularly. Don't worry about the bill," he added with a grin. "I trust you for it. We'll work something out. All right?"

"All right." She asked as many questions as she could, finding that knowledge was better than ignorance in such a situation. Then she went home and did what came naturally until her eyes were as red as her nose.

She laid her hand on the slight swell of her stomach and smiled through the tears. "Okay, buster, it's just you and me. I can't do it alone so you're going to have to help me. I want you, little one," she added with breathless tenderness. "You don't know how much! So will you try to stay alive, just for me?"

She laid her head back against the sofa and stared into space, her mind whirling with possibilities. No walking. No lifting. No strain of any kind. A quiet lifestyle, good food, no stress. That was pushing it for a single woman with no income, she mused. But she'd manage somehow. Women did, all over the world.

Telling Dane was out of the question, though. Even if he believed the baby was his, it would look as if she expected him to support her. It would mean living with him, letting him assume full responsibility for both of them. She couldn't do that to him. He didn't want commitment, he didn't want marriage. He'd said so forcefully when he'd thrown her out of his life, and she'd gone willingly. This was no time to open old wounds.

Someday, perhaps, she'd tell him, when she was back on her feet and no longer needed help. That way, she could go to him on an independent basis and let him decide if he wanted any part of the child's life.

That decided, she went and made herself a bowl of soup. There were all sorts of agencies to help expectant mothers, she knew. She'd just have to find one or two.

She quit her job the next day. Mr. Short was stunned. She explained that she had a bleeding ulcer—as good an excuse as any other lie, she thought miserably—and that her doctor had advised her to stop working for a couple of months. He was sympathetic and insisted on giving her two weeks severance pay, which was very good of him considering that she couldn't give notice and had left him shorthanded. She apologized profusely and went home to her apartment. She'd never felt so scared or alone in her life. Not that the baby wasn't going to be worth all the sacrifices, she assured herself. The baby would be her whole world!

She spent the next few days getting used to a new routine. She found a part-time job doing telephone sales from the apartment, which brought in a little income. She had enough money to pay the rent for three months, which she did to insure that she wouldn't get thrown out during the first part of her confinement. Since utilities were included in the rent, that was taken care of as well. One of the government agencies provided coupons for milk and cheese, to give the baby enough protein, and she arranged to make regular payments on Dr. Boswick's bill from what she brought in from telephone sales.

Meals were precarious. She made plenty of stews and casseroles to stretch her food budget, and took her prenatal vitamins regularly. The worst of it was being totally alone in the daytime. Her neighbors all worked, so there was no one she could call for help if she got into trouble.

She lost weight because of the strain and worry. There were still periods of spotting, when she had to call Dr. Boswick, and every episode meant days in bed until the bleeding stopped. She had to take extra iron tablets to compensate for the loss of blood. She was tired all the time.

Kit came to see her, bringing tasty things to tempt her appetite. Tess had sworn her to secrecy, and she stopped answering the phone so that nobody from Dane's office could reach her.

But if she thought those measures would discourage anyone from checking up on her sudden retirement from work, she was mistaken.

She woke to the sound of the doorbell being jabbed repeatedly early one rainy morning two weeks later. Morning sickness still plagued her. She'd just returned from the bathroom and another bout of nausea. She was bundled up in her thick red bathrobe over striped pajamas, her hair tousled and needing cutting badly. She looked terrible. When she opened the door, annoyed at the repeated buzzing, she came face to face with Dane. He was more startled than she was.

"My God!" he swore slowly, his breath catching as he looked at her.

"Thanks, you look wonderful, too," she muttered weakly. "You'll have to let yourself in. I have to get back to bed before I fall down."

"Wait. I'll carry you."

He closed the door and picked her up before she could protest, hefting her easily against his chest. He frowned as he carried her into the bedroom. His back protested for the first time in memory, but he didn't let on to the fact. "You've gained weight again, or is it swelling from the ulcer?" He laid her gently on the bed and started to remove the robe.

She couldn't risk having him see her body, so she caught his fingers. "I'm cold, leave it on," she said huskily.

"Okay." He pulled the covers over her and sat down beside her, his eyes dark with concern. "Short told me you'd quit. Are you getting treatment, for God's sake?"

She stared at him, feeling alone and frightened, a sense of hopelessness in her eyes. He looked very successful in his charcoal gray suit, with a red-and-black striped tie and a matching handkerchief in his watch pocket. By comparison, she looked like something the cat had brought in.

"Treatment?" she asked absently. She grimaced and tears gathered hotly in her eyes. "There is no treatment," she whispered huskily. "The doctor's already done all he can do."

He scowled. "For a bleeding ulcer?"

"It isn't a bleeding ulcer," she said dully, closing her eyes.

He stilled. "Then what is it?"

"Nothing that can be cured with a pill, I'm afraid," she said tiredly. "Dane, I'm so tired . . . !"

"What do you have?" he asked with concern he couldn't hide. He looked pale, she thought. Then she realized what he must be thinking.

"Oh," she said, her mind finally grasping what h€ thought. "No, it's not cancer. I'm not dying. Really I'n not. I don't have anything terminal."

He let out a heavy breath and fumbled in his pocket for a cigarette. "God, you scared me to death," he ground out "If it's not that, and not a bleeding ulcer, what did yo mean there's nothing they can do?"

She hesitated. Now that he was here, she wanted to tel him. She was afraid and alone, and she wanted to lean o: him, to be taken care of, protected. She wanted him to knov about the child. But would it be fair to tell him? Now, whe: she was so close to losing it?

He saw the tormented look in her eyes without under standing it. He touched her dull hair curiously. "You loo terrible," he said. He studied her narrowly. "Are you gc ing to tell me what's the matter with you, Tess?"

She nibbled on her lower lip. "I don't know if I should, she said honestly. "You may not believe me. Even if you d€ I'm not sure it's fair."

He looked at her with quiet contentment. Even when sh was half-dead with illness, he felt at home with her. A peace. He smoothed her hair away from her forehead. "A the color is gone, did you know?" he asked quietly. "I g€ up, I go to work, I go home and I lie awake at night. I don care about the job, or much else. You took the joy out c living when you went away."

"You sent me away," she said softly.

He searched her pained eyes. "Yes. I didn't want an thing permanent...."

"I haven't asked for anything permanent," she inte rupted. "You don't have to worry that I would. I'm n€ asking for anything now, although it might sound like it, guess."

He scowled. "Explain that."

She took a deep breath and met his eyes reluctantly. "Dane... I'm pregnant."

The look on his face might, in other circumstances have been comical. He stopped with the cigarette an inch from his mouth and stared at her like a man who'd been bashed in the head with a shovel.

He lowered the cigarette very slowly and without thinking dropped it into a glass of water on the bedside table. "You're what?" he asked in a choked tone.

"I'm going to have a baby."

Something in his expression made her nervous. He looked ill. His eyes glittered in a countenance that seemed carved out of stone. Slowly, slowly, his gaze moved down her body. He reached out, drawing the covers away. His hands found the tie of the robe and loosened it. He pulled the thick red fabric away from her body and unsnapped the catch of her pajama pants before she could protest. Then he peeled them back from the slight, swollen softness of her stomach and sat staring at it like a demented man.

"You didn't tell me," he said roughly.

"I didn't know how," she groaned. Her anguished eyes searched his face.

Slowly, he stretched both his lean, warm hands toward her belly and touched it. There was something reverent about the way he did it, about the hushed rasp of his breathing. He lifted his dark eyes to hers and his cheekbones flushed with building temper.

"I thought I couldn't father a child. You knew that. God in heaven, how could you have kept it from me?"

She hesitated. "I'm sorry," she said, too shaken by his reaction to try to explain her reasoning.

"Sorry...!" He bit off what he was going to say as the enormity of her condition got through to him. "When is he due?" he asked, glaring at her. "How soon?"

She managed to meet his stormy eyes. "Five months."
She hesitated, indecision tearing her apart. His face was livid
with his discovery, with the pleasure he couldn't hide of
knowing that he'd fathered her child. How could she destroy his peace of mind, now? But she had to give some excuse for staying home, for her inactivity. She bit her lip.
"Dane..." She swallowed. "I have to stay at home until I
deliver. I can't work."

"Why?" he asked curtly.

She hesitated. Her eyes adored him involuntarily. She
loved him far too much to tell him how dangerous the pregnancy was, how much risk was involved. Fear for the child
would drive him mad.

"I'm having a lot of morning sickness," she hedged.

"I see." Obviously relieved, he let out a sigh.

He got up from the bed and turned away, running a restless hand around the back of his neck as he stared blindly at
the wall.

"You don't have to feel responsible," she said helplessly

"Don't be absurd. It's my baby." He turned, his face
slowly changing with dawning wonder as he looked down at
her. "My baby," he repeated slowly, his eyes on her stomach. He smiled faintly. Then his dark eyes cut at her. "And
you weren't even going to tell me, damn you!"

She cringed at his tone. But it was either let him believe
that, or force him to share her quiet terror. He'd been
through so much in the past few years. His mother's death
his horrible injury in the shooting, the loss of his job. No
she thought with helpless compassion, no, not this, too. She
lifted her face bravely. "You said you didn't want commit
ment, remember?" she asked coolly. "You wanted me ou
of your life. If I'd told you about the baby, you'd have
thought I was trying to trap you," she said instead.

The accusation made him feel guilty. She didn't know
how he really felt. She looked indifferent, and he wasn'

onfident about revealing his emotions right now. He'd told
er he didn't want commitment, sure, but that was when he
hought he couldn't give her a full marriage. Now he could,
ut she didn't seem to want him anymore.

He drew back into himself. It was the child he had to be
oncerned with now. Later, he and Tess could sort them-
elves out. First things first. "Things have changed," he said
uietly.

"You mean you didn't want me, but the baby is another
natter."

Her expression kindled his temper. "Of course," he said
vith a mocking smile, lashing out at her.

She stared at him with a breaking heart, but she didn't
are let him know how much that flat statement had hurt.

"Did you ever plan to tell me?" he persisted.

"Yes," she said. "Eventually."

"When?" he drawled, his black eyes accusing. "After he
tarted school? Well, you don't need to tell me now. I
now." He stuck a lean hand in his slacks pocket and stared
t her, refusing to let his emotions show. Her treachery in
iding her condition from him, when she knew he thought
e was sterile, was going to take some forgiveness, but that
night come in time. "I'll take you down to the ranch," he
aid, thinking out loud. "You'll have Beryl for company."

"No," she murmured, averting her eyes. "I—can't go
here."

He frowned. Then he remembered what he'd told her
bout Beryl. They weren't married and she was pregnant.

Inside, he brightened. Now he had a concrete reason for
narrying her, one that spared him from revealing his real
eelings. Let her think it was only because of the child.

"We'll work out something." He flicked his cuff back and
ooked at his watch, his mind churning. "I'll be back in a
ew minutes."

"Dane, we have to talk," she began.

"Later."

He glanced at her again with quiet possessiveness, but he didn't speak. He left the apartment and Tess lay back, disturbed and saddened by the way he was acting. He'd admitted that the child was all he wanted. She'd hoped he might have missed her, wanted her back, but that was daydreaming.

If his appearance in her life had been a shock, what he came back with three hours later was devastating. He dragged a strange man into the room with him, handed her a pen and a sheet of paper and indicated where she was to sign it and how. He didn't even give her time to read it before he laid it on the table and sat down beside her, taking her hand in his.

"Go ahead," he told the man.

The man produced a small book, smiled, and proceeded to read a wedding service. Tess was so shocked that she was barely able to answer when called upon. Before she knew it Dane was sliding a plain gold band—two sizes too big—on her finger, and she was married.

"Dane...!" she protested.

He got up and shook hands with the man, let him sign the paper, handed him a wad of bills and escorted him to the door with profuse thanks.

When he'd let him out, Dane moved back to the bed and looked down at Tess. She was his wife now. She belonged to him—she and the baby. His baby. His chest swelled with raging pride.

She looked at the ring on her finger dazedly, trying to equate it with the odd look on Dane's face, the glittery darkness of his eyes.

"It takes three...three days to get married...." she stammered.

"It takes one if you threaten to shoot a judge," he said pleasantly. "Don't worry, it's perfectly legal." He frowned houghtfully. "I don't know about the kidnapping charge, hough."

"What kidnapping?"

"The probate judge who just married us didn't know he vas going to," he explained. "I appropriated him at the courthouse and brought him with me."

She laughed. Then she cried. It was so unlike Dane to be mpulsive like that.

He cursed under his breath. "All right, I'm sorry I had to pring it on you without any warning," he said stiffly. "But ve had to present Beryl with a fait accompli when I take you here tonight."

"It isn't fair that she has to be responsible for me," she vhispered. "Or you, either, for that matter."

He lifted his head. "You have my baby inside you," he aid, his eyes darkening as he searched hers. It took all his villpower to keep himself from lifting her into his arms and cissing those tears away. "The baby is all that matters right low. My God, it's everything!" he breathed huskily.

He certainly did want the child, she thought sadly. She stared at his tie, wondering how he was going to feel if she ost it, if he ended up married to her for no reason. It would be so much worse, because she hadn't told him the truth. But how could she?

"Stop brooding," he said. "I'll take care of you, Miss Meriwether." He hesitated. "Mrs. Lassiter," he corrected. The name had a new sound, a different sound from when it had been used for Jane. "Mrs. Teresa Lassiter," he murmured.

She lifted her sad eyes to his. "You really do want the baby, don't you?"

His face went hard. "You know that already. Hadn't you realized how I felt, thinking that I couldn't father a child? Didn't it matter to you?"

She stiffened miserably. "Yes, it mattered...." She choked and shifted. "I didn't want you to feel trapped, or that you had to marry me," she said finally, giving him the only reason she felt safe disclosing. "I knew you didn't want to marry again. You'd said so half a dozen times."

He only looked at her, his eyes narrow and probing. That had been true, until he'd made such long, sweet love to her. After that, she'd become his world. The baby was a bonus, a big one, but it was her he'd wanted. He hadn't wanted to marry her and have her grieve for lack of a child. Jane's obsession to get pregnant had left deep scars on his emotions. They'd influenced his attitude toward Tess. Now, all he wanted was Tess. He wanted his child, too. But she'd meant to keep her conception a secret, and he didn't think it was because of the flimsy reason she'd given him. Did she hate him now—was that it? Had his treatment of her killed what she'd once felt for him? Uncertain, he withdrew behind a camouflage of anger.

"Whether or not I wanted to remarry is a moot point now, isn't it?" he asked, more harshly than he'd intended. "The child has to have a name. We'll get by, somehow."

That wasn't what she wanted to hear. She wanted him to say that he loved her desperately, that he'd want her even if she wasn't carrying his child, that he'd missed her and needed her. None of that was realistic, though. The truth was that he'd done very well without her. If not for the baby, he'd never have come near her again.

His presence in the restaurant that day was puzzling, though. Why had he been there? Kit had hinted that he'd wanted to see Tess. She didn't believe it. Dane knew where she lived. He could have seen her anytime. No, Kit was wrong. It had only been a coincidence. She'd looked bad and he'd felt sorry for her. She drooped a little, worn out from the emotional strain of the day.

"I want you to change clothes, if you can manage. Then we'll get your things together and go down to the ranch. I guess morning sickness can be pretty debilitating."

"Yes," she said evasively. "It can. I'd like to have a bath first," she said weakly.

"Are you up to it?"

She nodded. "The nausea is the worst when I first wake up. I'll be all right."

"Tell me what to pack and where to find it. I'll take care of that. If you need me, I'll be within earshot."

She did, amazed at how quickly he'd taken over. It was nice to have everything arranged, to be looked after. She was too weak and sick to take care of herself. She wouldn't think about his motives. If she did, she'd go crazy.

An hour later, bathed and dressed, she let Dane lead her out to the black Mercedes. He'd already talked to the landlord—God knew what he'd said—and her bags were packed and in the car.

She worried all the way to Branntville about what Beryl was going to say. Dane talked to her about work, about Helen and the staff, but she barely heard him. She was too upset to listen.

She needn't have worried. Beryl came out to the car to meet her, looking motherly.

"You poor child," she said gently, opening the door for her. "Don't you worry about a thing," she said sternly. "It's going to be all right. When Dane can't be here, I will. I won't let anything happen to you."

It was too much, after all the worry. She broke down, letting Beryl cuddle her while she cried her heart out.

"Here, this won't do," Dane said finally. He drew her away from Beryl and lifted her against him. "I'll carry you inside. You need to rest. It's been a long day."

"I'll warm up some of the nice chicken soup I made," Beryl promised. "You'll like it. It will be good for the baby," she added, her eyes twinkling as she went ahead of them.

"You told her?" Tess asked Dane.

"Yes." He searched her eyes. "Everything's all right. All you have to do is rest."

She nodded. But she was thinking that life wasn't that simple. It seemed suddenly very much harder than it had been, with the man she loved most in the world both so close and so far away, and her baby under constant threat. She wondered if she might go quietly mad.

Ten
___

Dane had his evening meal in the room with Tess. Beryl had helped her into a pair of clean pajamas and a matching robe, and had tucked her up in the big antique four-poster bed, sympathizing with Tess's incapacitating nausea. Tess felt guilty letting Beryl and Dane believe it was only that. But she'd have felt worse telling them the truth.

This wasn't the same bed she'd slept in the last time she'd been at the ranch, and it was in a different part of the sprawling house. She hadn't asked Beryl why she was in here, or if it was near Dane's room. She'd been too shy.

"Eat," he told her firmly, watching her toy with her spoon.

"Sorry. I was just wondering whose room this was."

"It's mine," he said quietly, watching her start. He nodded grimly. "That's right. You're sharing it with me."

She stared at him wildly. They couldn't be intimate, but how was she going to tell him that without telling him everything? "Dane..." she began worriedly after she'd lifted a spoonful of hot, delicious chicken soup to her mouth.

"I know that sex can be unpleasant for a pregnant woman," he said unexpectedly. "I want you with me at night, that's all. If you need me, I'll be close by."

His concern touched her, even as the flat statement about no intimacy reassured her. "Thank you."

He hated her look of relief. It made him feel unwanted, but he disguised his reaction. "Have you thought about names? Do you hope it's a boy or do you want a little girl?" he asked.

She'd been afraid to hope, but he couldn't know that. "No. I don't care if it's a boy or a girl."

"Neither do I," he replied. "As long as the baby's healthy, that's all that matters."

She nodded. "You were an only child, weren't you?" she said, desperate to change the subject.

"Yes, but my mother didn't really want me," he said bitterly, his eyes going dark with remembered pain.

"This baby will be wanted," she said softly.

His eyes lifted. He looked at her, sitting there so vulnerable and pretty in his bed, her blond hair soft and curling, her big gray eyes watching him. "He certainly will."

"Was your father an only child?"

"I don't know," he said. "He never talked about his family. He vanished when I was young, and I didn't hear from him again. My mother had two brothers, but they died in Vietnam, both of them."

"You and your mother never got along, even when you were a child?" she asked.

"No." He closed up. "Eat your soup."

She grimaced and went back to the nourishing liquid. He had a knack for closing doors, she thought.

They'd eaten fairly late. Dane took time to check with his ranch foreman before he came back into the bedroom and began stripping off his clothes.

Tess tried not to watch, but she couldn't help it. He was the most magnificent man she'd ever seen. Her eyes lingered on the deep scars on his back and shoulder before he turned, and then her attention was captured by the powerful lines of his arms and chest. She was so preoccupied that he'd taken off everything he was wearing before she became aware of it—and the fact that she was staring. She went scarlet.

He smiled faintly as he moved to turn off the lights. "You'll get used to me," he said, ignoring her scarlet blush. "I wore pajamas for your sake at the apartment, but we're married now. I've slept this way since I was a boy. Old habits are hard to part with."

"I don't mind," she said as he climbed in under the covers beside her. "It's your bedroom, after all."

"Know where the controls are for the electric blanket? It's spring, but the weather still turns cold sometimes at night."

"Yes, I found them earlier." She lay quietly under the soft warmth of the sheet and electric blanket, her eyes on the dark ceiling, trying not to move around and disturb him. This was familiar, because she'd slept with him once before. But then it had been new and exciting and she'd slept because of exhaustion. Now, it was difficult to get used to having someone beside her in the darkness. Not only that, she could feel his resentment, his displeasure.

His hand suddenly slid over her stomach and pressed there, making her jump.

"Don't have hysterics. I want to feel him. Does he move yet?"

She swallowed. The feel of his hand was comforting as much as disturbing. "Little flutters," she managed. "He'll start to kick soon."

"Are you going to nurse him, Tess?"

Her heart skipped. She thought about it, about the advantages of it that she'd read about in magazines. "Yes. I want to, very much."

She held her breath, hoping that he might pull her close and cradle her in his arms while she slept. But he didn't. He removed his hand and she felt him turn away form her. It was like a harbinger of things to come. It made her nervous.

She didn't know that he was concealing an explosion of emotions he didn't want her to sense. He felt like a magician when he thought of her pregnancy. He'd never wanted anything as much as he wanted this child; anything, except Tess herself. That was something he couldn't quite admit yet. His emotional scars were hurting. He'd thought he could trust Tess because she loved him, but she'd denied him the one miracle of his life—the knowledge of his paternity. If he hadn't gone looking for her, she wouldn't have told him. It didn't bear thinking about.

He closed his eyes with a rough sigh and finally slept.

From that night on, the distance between them grew. Tess became quiet and shy around him. At night he had to reach for her. She never went to him voluntarily, never teased him or played with him or looked at him with love in her eyes as she had months before. The baby began to kick, and she longed to share it with him, but she was too subdued to invite that intimacy. He never touched her these days. He talked about the future sometimes, but the conversation was always about the baby, never about Tess and himself.

Tess grew depressed. They seemed not to be able to communicate anymore. Tess helped Beryl work in the flower beds during the warm afternoons, but Dane soon noticed that she seemed to do nothing strenuous at all. She never exerted herself. That disturbed him, because exercise, he'd been told, made the delivery all that much easier.

"You don't do enough," he said one evening after he'd come home from work. "You sit around all day. I want you to start walking. No arguments," he said firmly when she started. "This inactivity isn't healthy for the child. Tomorrow when I get home, we'll take a nice turn around the ranch."

"Dane," she began nervously.

He glanced at his watch. "I'm on stakeout tonight. We'll talk later, Tess. Don't stay up too late. It isn't good for the baby."

She could have screamed. Everything he said or did was with the baby in mind. She was only the incubator, it seemed. Not that she wasn't concerned about her child; she was all too concerned. She hadn't told him the truth, and now things were going to get dangerous if he insisted on her walking. It could cause the bleeding to come back again.

She'd felt a revival of good health since she'd been with him. The pain had stopped, and the bleeding had stopped, too. She felt optimistic for the first time. But what he proposed could cost her the child. She worried all night about how or if to tell him the truth.

Fortunately, his stakeout extended for the next several days, and Tess learned to lie. Beryl went to help out an elderly neighbor an hour a day, and during her absence, Tess told Dane, she made sure that she walked.

He froze up, disturbed that she seemed to be making sure that he spent no time at all with her.

"Is my company that distasteful to you?" he demanded coldly, his smile no smile at all. "You can't bear having me near you, so you go walking when I'm not around, is that it?"

"No!"

"Well, don't sweat it, honey," he said icily. "It's the baby I'm concerned with, not you."

He'd lashed out in a moment of fury, but Tess didn't know that it was because she'd hurt him. She winced at the anger, at his flat statement that she didn't matter to him. It was no more than she'd expected, but it left a deep wound.

She turned away, her face lifted proudly. "I'll make sure the baby isn't harmed by my life-style."

"See that you do. Mrs. Lassiter," he added with venom.

She looked up at him, her eyes quietly accusing. "If I hadn't been pregnant, you'd never have married me, would you?"

"Didn't you know that already?" he agreed unsmilingly. "You're treacherous, Tess, like the rest of your sex. My mother drove my father away. She broke him, because he loved her. Jane very nearly did the same damned thing to me with her obsession to become pregnant, her distaste for my job. You were the last person in the world I'd have expected to put a knife in my back. My mistake. You won't get a second chance. Just be sure you don't harm my child," he said with cold authority.

"I didn't hide it from you to hurt you," she blurted.

He ignored that. "I'll be late for work."

"Why won't you talk to me?" she ground out. "You can't even be bothered to come home at night anymore. You're always gone."

He couldn't admit how hungry he was for her. He stayed away because the mask slipped sometimes when he looked at her, because he cared too much. "What is there to say?" he asked evasively. "You seduced me into your arms the night we made the baby. I gave in, because I wanted you. But it was only desire. You understand? Only that. Nothing more."

A light went out in her. "Yes, Dane," she said. "I understand."

She left the room, tears blinding her. He couldn't have made it any more plain than that.

He slammed his fist down on the dresser top in impotent rage. He hadn't meant to say that, to belittle the exquisite loving they'd shared. He didn't trust her. He couldn't. She was like his mother, like Jane. She was going to sell him out. In fact, she already had, by hiding her pregnancy. She didn't love him now. She avoided him, never looked at him. The baby was all she seemed interested in. He had to remember that and not weaken again. But it was hard. He adored her, never more than now, as she blossomed with his child. It should have been a time of sharing, of unequaled closeness. But he withdrew, because she pushed him away. Nothing had ever hurt quite so much.

Weeks turned to months. Dane and Tess lived like polite strangers. He'd long since moved her into another bedroom, with the excuse that he was disturbing her sleep with his late hours. It wasn't true. Her silence, her depression was disturbing him. She looked at him with an expression he couldn't fathom, as if she were hurting and hiding it. He felt guilty every time he saw her and he didn't know why. Being near her and unable to touch her, to hold her, was killing him. He sat and stared at her when she wasn't looking, like a lovesick boy. His work suffered because he couldn't keep his mind off her. She grew bigger and paler, and one day, after she'd been to see her obstetrician, she took to her bed and stayed there. That disturbed him, and he said something about it.

"Are you all right?" he asked her that evening, his eyes concerned.

"Of course," she replied, her face schooled to disguise her terror. She'd had a lot of bleeding and Dr. Boswick was worried. He didn't say so, but his expression hadn't been reassuring. She was scared and she wanted to tell Dane, but it was far too late for that. "I'm just tired. There's so much of me to carry around," she added impotently.

"I told you before," he said quietly, "that I don't want you lying around the house. You have to get enough exercise. I'm sure the obstetrician's told you that."

She felt near panic. It was fall now and good walking weather, but she didn't dare! Dane was still irritable since she'd refused to go to natural childbirth classes with him. She was too afraid of the trips to and from the hospital where they were given, because what Dr. Boswick had told her about the final trimester unnerved her. He had said the method might help, but he hadn't pressured her to attend the classes. He knew how afraid she was.

Her visits to the obstetrician had been very close together lately, and fortunately, Dane didn't know why. She'd managed to keep her secret, despite his cold indifference to her feelings. She'd protected him from the fear. She knew all too well how much a child would mean to him. She wanted him to have his son—Dr. Boswick had told her that it would be a boy.

She looked up at Dane from her reclining position on the bed, propped up by pillows because she was so big now, in her eighth month.

"I'll go walking tomorrow," she promised. "It's so hard these days. I'm heavier than I've ever been."

His dark eyes narrowed on her wan, pinched face. He felt guilty all over again, just looking at her. "Why is it that I never see you walk?" he asked. "You always arrange to do it when no one is here except you."

She colored and averted his eyes.

"I know you're heavy. But, Tess, laziness is no excuse," he said quietly. "This is for your own good. Tomorrow, you walk. I'll make sure of it."

"No," she replied wearily, tired of the deception. "No, I can't do that." She took a deep breath. "Dane, there's something I haven't told you, something you need to know.... Oh!" She gasped at the wrenching pain that caught her unaware and lifted her straight up on the bed. She cried out piteously.

"The baby!" he exclaimed harshly. "Tess, is it the baby?"

"Yes...!" She wept because the sudden contractions were so fierce. Even as she felt them, she felt a terrifying gush of wet warmth beneath her and her face went stark white. "You have...to get...an ambulance! Call Dr. Boswick...!"

"It may be false labor. You're a month early. I'll take you in the car," he began tersely, and threw back the covers.

He froze. Every drop of color ran out of his face, every sign of life. His black eyes glittered like diamond fragments. "Oh, my God!" he exploded.

"Call...an ambulance!" she cried.

He grabbed up the telephone by the bed, galvanized into action. Beryl came running while he was talking to the hospital and, seeing the situation for herself, went running to get towels.

Assured that an ambulance was already in their end of the county and could be there in five minutes, he dialed Dr. Boswick.

"I think there's something wrong. She's in pain and bleeding badly," Dane said, his voice cold but unsteady. "The ambulance is on the way."

"The placenta has detached," came the terse reply. "When I examined her today, I warned her that it could happen any time. The baby is near enough to term that it has a chance, but we could still lose both of them," he said, and Dane's heart stopped. "She hasn't been exercising today?"

Dane's fingers shook on the receiver. "No."

"Thank God for that. I'm sure she's told you how dangerous her condition is, so that you wouldn't allow her to exert unnecessarily. I'll be at the emergency room when they bring her in, and we'll gear up for a transfusion." He told Dane what to do, to help contain the bleeding. "Tell those paramedics that every second counts."

Dane hung up, tossing orders to Beryl. He looked down at Tess with anguished realization.

"Something went wrong a long time ago, didn't it? It's been there all along. It wasn't morning sickness that kept you home at all," he ground out, his voice tormented.

Her lips were white as she compressed them, trying not to scream from the pain. "You wanted...the baby...so much," she panted. "I only wanted...to spare you," she whispered weakly. "Not...your fault!"

"So you took the risk and the worry all alone, and I gave you hell.... Oh, God, Tess...!" His voice broke. He touched her face with unsteady fingers, as she arched and cried out again from the force of the pain.

"Where the hell is that ambulance?" he cursed.

A faint sound of sirens was barely audible as Tess caught her breath. "Hold on, little one," he said huskily, motioning for Beryl to stay with her. He went out of the room as the sirens approached, so shaken that he could hardly speak at all.

Tess was barely conscious on the long drive to the hospital. Dane sat beside her in a terrified posture while the ambulance attendants kept watch on her and did what they could to stem the profuse bleeding. Dr. Boswick was waiting when they wheeled her into Branntville General.

"She comes first," Dane told the doctor, white-faced. "No matter what, she comes first, do you understand?"

"We'll do everything we can," Boswick assured him. They rushed her to the operating room and, minutes later, took the baby.

She was drifting through layers of pain and drug-induced drowsiness when she heard a voice at her ear.

"It's a boy," Dane whispered. "Can you hear me, sweetheart? We have a little boy."

She barely made sense of the words. "John Richard," she whispered with difficulty.

It was the name they'd both chosen for a boy, on one of the rare evenings when he'd been home on time and they'd talked. He touched her mouth with his. "John Richard," he whispered. "How do you feel, darling?"

That couldn't be Dane calling her darling. She must be delirious. "Hurts," she said weakly.

"They'll give you something else. The nurse is bringing a shot for you. He's so beautiful, Tess," he said unsteadily. "So beautiful."

Her eyes opened, glazed with pain. She looked up at him. "Love...you," she managed. "Whatever happens...always remember."

His eyes were wet. She couldn't see them clearly, but she heard the rough sound he made.

"You're going to be all right," he said harshly. "They said so. Don't talk like that!"

Her eyelids were so heavy. She felt them close. "Take care of him," she said weakly. "You wanted him...so much."

"I want you!" He leaned close, his voice in her ear. "Listen to me, you silly child, I lied! I've been lying all along! I didn't think I could give you a child—that's why I didn't want to marry you! It was for your sake, not mine, that I let you go! Tess, it's you I want! You! God in Heaven, I almost went out of my mind when Dr. Boswick told me about your condition after they took the baby. Open your eyes, Tess. Open your eyes!"

He sounded urgent, almost desperate. She forced her eyelids open again with an effort and tried to focus. His face was white. Stark white.

"Don't you die on me!" he said through his teeth. "Don't you dare! You're going to live and help me raise our baby.

I'm not going to try and live without you again! I can't. Listen to me—I can't make it without you!''

"Only...the baby...you want," she managed.

"No."

Nothing he said was getting through the pain. "Yes. You said..."

He realized that she wasn't comprehending any of it. He had to make her listen, make her understand, while there was still time! "Look at me. Tess, look at me. Look at me!"

She swallowed, forcing her eyes toward his face.

"I love you." He said each word deliberately, forcefully. His eyes were blazing like black coals in his face. "I love you!"

That was nice. She tried to say so, but darkness fell on her like a wall. She closed her eyes, and the anguished sound of his voice slowly became indistinguishable. She slept.

Eleven

Dane sat beside her all night without sleeping. He couldn't bring himself to leave her, not even to see the son he'd thought he'd never have.

Her face was pale and she cried out with the pain, even with the sedatives they were giving her. He watched her suffer, and suffered with her. It devastated him to know what she'd gone through in such silence, sparing him from the worry that had haunted her all these long months. He'd accused her of betraying him, when she was in fact protecting him. She'd loved him and he'd failed her at every turn, when he loved her more than his own life.

But she didn't know that. He'd said so many cruel things to her. She might not be able to forgive him, but she had to stay alive. She had to!

Daylight was streaming in the windows and the hospital was bustling with activity when she finally came back to consciousness. She was weak and still in pain.

She opened her eyes. "Dane?" she whispered. "My baby...?"

He looked terrible, she thought dimly. His face was unshaven and starkly lined.

"Do you want the baby now?" he asked gently, bending over her. "They'll bring him whenever you like. Right now, if you want."

She swallowed. "I want to see him."

He pushed the buzzer and called the nurse, asking for John to be brought in. The cheerful voice promised instant compliance. Sure enough, barely two minutes later, a nurse came into the room with a small bundle in her arms.

"Here he is, Mrs. Lassiter," the nurse said cheerfully. "I'm glad to see you awake. You had us worried for a little while. Look what I've got."

She laid the bundle down beside Tess and pulled the blanket away from the baby's face.

Tess looked at him and saw Dane. She caught her breath. "He looks like my husband," she whispered. "Oh, he looks like you, Dane!"

He leaned over her, touching the baby's head gently. "He has your eyes," he disagreed. "Big and soft."

"I'll bring his bottle—" the nurse began.

"No," Tess protested. She looked up. "Please. I want to feed him myself. Dr. Boswick said—"

"All right." The nurse smiled. "We'll bring the bottle, too. You're very weak. You lost a lot of blood, and you may not have enough milk yet to satisfy him."

The nurse went out and Tess fought pain to sit up against the pillows with the baby in her arms. "Help me, please," she whispered, tugging at the neck of the gown.

He found the ties and helped her ease the gown away. She brought the baby to her breast and gently nudged the nipple into his mouth. He began to suckle at once, his tiny hand clenched against her breast.

She caught her breath at the pins-and-needles sensation, and then she laughed. She looked up at Dane, but he wasn't laughing. His face was rigid and ruddy with color as he watched. His jaw clenched.

"My God," he said unsteadily. "I didn't realize it would look like that." He moved closer, his eyes helplessly riveted to the baby. He reached down and lightly touched the small head before he looked into Tess's eyes. "Does it hurt you?" he asked.

"No," she said. "It's uncomfortable just at first, that's all. My stomach feels awful," she grimaced. "The stitches pull and it hurts."

"They can give you something else when you're finished with John Richard."

"You aren't at work," she said, frowning.

"I couldn't leave you, honey," he replied quietly. "You scared me."

"Scared you?"

He hesitated for a long moment before he spoke. "You sounded as if you meant to go away," he said. His hand touched her mouth. "I was afraid you didn't want to live."

"I don't remember."

"It could have been the drugs, but I couldn't take a chance." He bent and kissed her gently. "You mean the world to me," he said huskily. "I can't lose you now."

She didn't trust her ears, or her mind. She only smiled, certain that it was the first flush of new fatherhood talking. Whatever he felt, he wanted John, and since there was no other woman in his life, presumably he'd decided that they might as well stay married. She'd take a chance on him, she decided. After all, he might learn to love her one day.

A week later, she and John were released from the hospital. Helen and Kit came to see the baby, raving over him while Tess smiled indulgently.

Dane was always somewhere nearby, although he went back to work with a vengeance. Tess was aware of his irritation that she wouldn't listen to him when he tried to talk to her. She couldn't help it. She didn't want him making confessions of love. He'd been upset about her condition once he found out about it, and the labor had been a nightmare. Now he was feeling elated with his new son and relieved that Tess was out of danger. He was happy. But Tess didn't want any false promises. She wanted him cold sober and completely over the experience of her pregnancy before they talked again.

Meanwhile, she had her son to take care of. It was six weeks before she could get around enough to feel like her old self. She doted on the baby, adored him, cosseted him, spent every free second with him. The baby was her life.

He was Dane's, too, but as Tess lavished attention on the child, she denied it to him. He began to feel alone, unwanted, and his temper became hot and unpredictable. He loved his son, but he couldn't seem to make Tess notice that he needed her, too. She'd withdrawn into a world of her own, where her child was the only other occupant.

She was feeding John early one Saturday afternoon when Dane came down the hall, his gloves clenched in one hand, his chaps making leathery sounds against his powerful legs as he walked. His battered gray Stetson was cocked low over one eye. He wasn't working today, so he'd been out with his men on the ranch. He looked out of sorts and viciously irritable.

Dane paused in the doorway, hesitating as he saw Tess in the rocking chair in their bedroom, nursing the baby.

"I have to talk to you," he said tersely.

"I'll be finished in a minute," she replied.

He sat down on the edge of the bed, his eyes calming as he watched their child nurse. Pride softened his expression, and he smiled. "I never get tired of watching that," he said quietly. "You look like something out of a dream with the boy at your breast."

She smiled shyly. "He's growing, have you noticed?"

"Tess, how long are you going to nurse him?"

The question startled her. She looked up, idly brushing away a loosened strand of blond hair. She seemed so young in her green gingham dress, so vulnerable.

"I hadn't thought about it," she said. "Does it matter?"

He hesitated. "He's tied to you as long as you feed him," he said. "You can't be away from him for more than a couple of hours at a time."

Her face paled. Her eyes went huge in her face. "You want me to leave?" she asked huskily. "Is that why you want me to stop nursing him, so that you can get a nurse for him . . . ?"

His breathing checked. "God in heaven, no!"

She shivered, her expression torn between relief and fear.

He closed his eyes and reopened them. He got up and went to the window, slapping his gloves into his palm as he stared angrily out at the autumn landscape.

"I guess I've given you plenty of reason to think I wanted the baby and not you. But I'm not such a monster that I'd take your child away from you."

"I know that," she said, faintly shy of him. The baby finished pulling at her breast, his eyes drooping. She burped him and got up to put him in his baby bed against the wall, gently settling him on his side and covering him with a light blanket. She tiptoed out of the room, leaving Dane to follow.

"Don't run off again," he said tersely, glaring at her. "You've avoided me ever since you've been home."

"I want to sit on the porch," she said evasively.

"It's too cold."

"No, it isn't. I'll ask Beryl to watch out for John."

He gave in. "All right." He waited until she talked to Beryl, then he followed her out the back door and sat down beside her on the warm concrete stoop that overlooked the outbuildings.

She glanced at his batwing chaps. "You've been working."

"I bought some new horses," he said. "I've been watching the vet work on them."

He lit a cigarette and she stared out over the pasture.

"Tess, I've been trying to get you still long enough to apologize. I said some harsh, cruel things before the baby came. Things that haunt me now."

"You didn't know about what was wrong with me," she said simply. "I only wanted to spare you. You didn't think you could even have a child, and you were so excited about him." She smiled wanly. "I didn't want to spoil it for you."

His eyes closed and he groaned. "And what about you, you little idiot? Worried to death, and all you got from me was a cold shoulder and accusations about being lazy. Lazy!" He jerked off his hat and tossed it aside, running a restless hand through his hair. "I can't bear to remember the way I treated you. I've given you nothing but heartache, Tess."

She searched his profile quietly, her eyes soft and loving. "That isn't quite true. You gave me John."

He glanced down at her. "I never thought of precautions," he said slowly. "Because I didn't think I needed to. If I'd known the risk . . . !"

"But you didn't. Neither did I. But I would have taken the risk, even if I had known, Dane," she said with quiet conviction. "I'd do it all over again."

He searched her eyes slowly. "It wasn't just the baby I wanted," he said huskily. "It was you. I wanted you, needed you, so I . . . would have married you even if there hadn't been a child, because my world collapsed when you walked out of it. Sending you away was the single worst mistake of my life." His expression was vulnerable then, so loving that it knocked the breath out of her. "That night... I never knew what love was until then. I was afraid of it, terrified that I was wrong and it wouldn't last. But it has. It will. God, Tess," he whispered, "I'll love you until I die."

She shifted a little away from him and averted her eyes to the horizon. She couldn't believe him. She didn't dare. "You don't have to pretend," she said gently. "It's all right. You love John, and maybe you're fond of me. That will be enough."

He crushed out the cigarette and stood up. He glared at her. "No, it will not. You want me to love you."

She flushed and averted her gaze to the distant horizon. "I know how hard relationships are for you...."

He caught her gently by the shoulders and she stood up. "My mother warped my outlook. Jane savaged my pride. By the time you came along, I was an emotional basket case. I was afraid of you," he said. "Didn't you know?"

"I think part of me did." She lifted her eyes to his. "I tried to make you see that I'd never hurt you. But you wouldn't trust me."

"I couldn't." His hands slid down to clasp hers. "I told you that I didn't know how to love, how to be gentle." He leaned closer. "I had to learn those things. I learned them with you, Tess."

"You're proud of John," she whispered, glancing down, "and you felt responsible for the trouble I had. You don't have to say these things...."

He caught her chin between his thumb and forefinger and lifted her face, made her look at him. "I love you," he said. "How many ways, how many times, do I have to repeat it before you start believing that I mean it?"

She winced. Her eyes narrowed worriedly. "It might be so many things besides love, Dane."

"It might. But it isn't. You know it, you little coward." He smiled as he bent his head and gently took her lips with his. "But maybe it's time I proved it."

He kissed her softly, teasing her mouth until she began to relax, her mouth answering his in the warm silence of the afternoon. He caught his breath and groaned when he felt her arms go around him, felt the soft trembling of her body as she gave in. His lips probed her open mouth, his tongue teasing and then thrusting, so that she moaned hoarsely and tried to get closer to him.

His lean hand contracted at the base of her spine, rubbing her hungrily against his fierce arousal.

"I want you," he ground out. "Are you able?"

"Oh...yes," she whispered dazedly thorugh swollen lips, her body already throbbing wildly from the contact.

He groaned. "Where the hell can we go?" He lifted his head, looking so haunted that she almost smiled. "Beryl's upstairs with the baby."

She glanced toward the barn. He shook his head. "No," he said unsteadily. "It's far too unsanitary."

"They do it in books," she moaned.

"That is fantasy," he whispered. He nuzzled his face against her full breasts and then back up to her mouth. "And what I feel right now isn't a quick lust that I need to satisfy. I love you. I want to make love with you, be a part of you."

"I want that, too," she said huskily.

He pulled her closer, kissing her again, his mouth slow and sensuous, loving. "Tess," he breathed into her mouth, and he shuddered. "Tess, I love you...!"

The back door suddenly opened, breaking them apart, and Beryl came out wearing a sweater. "John's sleeping soundly. Would you two mind if I ran down to see about Mrs. Jewell? I'll only be an hour or so...."

Tess could have hugged her. She probably knew that the two of them would have killed for some time alone together, even with a sleeping baby nearby. "You go right ahead," Tess said softly.

"Thanks. Mrs. Jewell looks forward to our afternoons," Beryl assured her. She left, smiling secretly to herself.

They waited until the car pulled out of the driveway before Dane escorted her upstairs with undue haste and locked the bedroom door behind them.

He lifted her quickly and carried her to the bed, easing down onto it with her. "Don't be noisy or you'll wake the baby," he breathed into her mouth. "God bless Beryl...."

"The door..." She choked.

"It's locked. Tess, it's been so long!"

He kissed her with aching hunger for a long time until the fever burned too high to contain. He smiled sensually as he proceeded to remove every stitch of fabric from his powerful body. Tess watched him unashamedly, her eyes wide and curious. He was beautifully made, she thought, scars and all. The most perfect man she could ever have imagined.

As she thought it, she said it, whispered it to him. He smiled as he eased back down beside her and removed her dress and underthings between soft kisses.

She was a little self-conscious about her own scar, but he kissed it gently and smiled. It was, he murmured, like a battle scar that she'd earned with exceptional courage. She relaxed then and smiled back, lifting her face for his kiss.

She couldn't have imagined the tenderness of his possession. It was slow and thorough and breathlessly gentle. In between kisses and erotic caresses, he told her that he loved her, that he needed her, that she was the most important thing in his life. The magic they'd shared in his apartment was still there, intensified. He touched her and she felt boneless, anguished with her need of him.

Her arms clung to his neck when he moved over her and hesitated.

"Wait," he whispered. He paused and removed something he'd stuffed under a pillow, taking time to put it in place. She stared at him shyly. "No more babies just yet, sweetheart," he whispered softly. "I won't let you take that risk again."

"I'm all right," she said unsteadily. "It was a rare thing, Dane, and it might never happen again."

"We'll talk about it another time. You're weak and vulnerable right now. I have to take very good care of you, Mrs. Lassiter," he whispered against her mouth. "I love you far too much to risk losing you twice." He moved over her, easing her body to accommodate him. Then he began to join his body to hers with exquisite slowness and tenderness.

She was uncomfortable at first and he had to pause, to give her time to absorb him.

"You're like a virgin all over again," he said huskily, shivering with the restraint he was exercising for her sake. "Relax. Relax, little one. Yes." He sighed and let his hips slowly merge with hers.

She moaned as he completed his possession, her arms clinging as she lifted to him. "Oh, Dane," she gasped, "it's been almost a year...."

"I know," he said with a heavy groan, and his body began to move with helpless urgency.

She laughed in spite of the pleasure and kissed him hungrily. He caught her hips in his hands, and in seconds she was incapable of laughter or speech.

It was like the night they'd made the baby. She wept in his arms as the rhythm built in her body and in her blood, his possession of her so achingly complete that she went rigid with pleasure and stopped breathing altogether when the first heated contractions shook her under his weight. He cried out as she went over the edge, and her eyes opened at that instant, misty with her own helpless fulfillment. She saw him arch and his face clench just before her senses exploded, and she heard her own voice shattering....

She knew they'd never achieved such pleasure before. She lay heavily against his warm, damp body when they were coherent again, listening to his steady heartbeat, feeling him breathe against her breasts.

"You love me," he said with shaky humor. "I'd know it now even if you hadn't said it twenty times while we were loving just now."

"You said it several times yourself," she gasped.

He drew her closer and kissed her tenderly. "I mean it," he said. "Do you believe me now?"

She looked up into his soft, dark eyes. "Oh, yes," she agreed breathlessly, and blushed as she remembered the way it had been.

He bent and kissed her again with tenderness and possession. "I'd love to show you again, and again, and again," he whispered huskily. "But I hear the beginnings of a small thunderstorm."

She closed her eyes as he kissed her eyelids. "A small what?" She smiled lovingly.

"Listen."

A tiny sound exploded suddenly into a wail of pure fury in the quiet bedroom.

"Are you hungry again?" she asked, aghast. She threw her dress back on and got up to look at little John, who was waving his tiny fists and turning puce. "Or are you wet?"

"Better check for yourself," he murmured dryly from the bed. "As smart as he is, I doubt he's mastered enough English to answer you just yet."

She stuck out her tongue and proceeded to change a very wet diaper. As she was working on that, the telephone rang and Dane reached lazily across to answer it.

"No, I'm not coming in today. Why?" he asked. He frowned. Then he burst out laughing. "You don't mean it? When? Is she going to be all right?" He shook his head. "My God, of course I'll tell Tess. She'll die laughing. Tell her we'll be along to see her tonight, and for God's sake, confiscate her piece before she manages to do it again!"

"What is it?" Tess asked the minute he hung up.

"You'll never believe this," he said. He got up and pulled on his jeans, still chuckling. "You remember Helen was complaining that she was the only person in the office who'd never had a brush with a bullet?"

Her hands hesitated on the diaper she was fastening. "Yes."

"Well, it seems this afternoon she grabbed the wrong way for her pistol and shot herself in the foot."

"Oh, the poor thing!" Tess exclaimed, and ruined her sympathetic remark by bursting into helpless laughter. "I'm sorry, it isn't funny. She'll be all right?"

"Only a flesh wound. By the time she gets through embroidering it, she'll have had near-gangrene. They're keeping her overnight at the hospital just in case, so I told Nick we'd drop by to see her."

"I'll take flowers," she said. She grinned. "And a medal if we can find one."

He went to stand beside her as she finished changing the baby and lifted him into her arms. His eyes as he looked down at the two most beloved people in his life were stormy with happiness and love.

"He really does look like you," she said softly.

"Like both of us," he corrected, sliding a loving arm around her. His eyes twinkled. "Happy?"

"I never dreamed of being so happy." She reached up and kissed him. "You're not sorry it worked out this way, that you had to marry me?" she asked worriedly.

"I never *had* to marry you," he corrected with lazy tenderness. "I was only looking for an excuse, or did you really think I just happened into that restaurant the day you were having lunch with Kit?"

"You followed her!" she said, laughing. "She said you did."

"I followed her, all right. I'd brooded all morning about what I was going to do. Tess, I was going to ask you to come back with me," he confessed. "To live with me, marry me, to take a chance on a life without children."

She touched his face. "Oh, Dane!" she breathed.

"Then everything went wrong," he murmured. "And I got interrupted too soon."

"I was going to tell you about the baby," she replied, "and that man who approached you cost me my nerve."

He groaned. "All that time, wasted." He scowled suddenly. "You were having problems that day. It wasn't the ulcer, it was the baby."

"Yes," she said quietly. "But when you held my hand, the pain went away. I thought later that it was as if the baby knew you were his father, and he was responding to you."

His eyes darkened as he looked at her. "I gave you a hard time. I'm sorry, about everything."

"I loved you," she whispered. "I thought you might learn to love me, if I didn't rush you. I didn't want you to worry, or I'd have told you about the baby as soon as I knew. I didn't realize how hungry you really were for a child."

"Not for *a* child. For *our* child. Part of us." He bent and brushed his lips tenderly over the baby's temple, then he lifted his eyes back to hers. "You don't know how I missed you when you moved out of the apartment, or how afraid I was for you when those drug dealers were after you. For a long time, I thought I didn't want marriage. And then you wanted me to show you what lovemaking was." He groaned. "I didn't think it was possible to feel so deeply. I'd have done anything to get you, except sacrifice your need for a child." He searched her eyes. "It makes me humble, thinking of how much you were willing to sacrifice for me."

"Didn't that work both ways," she whispered.

He kissed her softly. "I like learning about love with you. I must be an apt pupil, because you sure make a lot of noise when we're in bed together."

She flushed, and he chuckled at her embarrassment. He grinned, bending to kiss her nose. "The baby gave me the best excuse in the world to marry you and take you home with me, without having to tell you how desperately I loved you. I thought I'd killed everything you felt for me."

"Silly man," she said lovingly. "Love doesn't die that easily."

"So it would seem. You had a hard time carrying John. Next time, we'll plan the baby, and I'll be with you every step of the way."

"That sounds like you want me to stop seducing you," she remarked.

"Heaven forbid!"

She smiled. "I wanted you so badly that night. I loved you. I thought if I gave you all I had to give and asked for nothing in return, you might learn to trust me, maybe to love me."

"I loved you, all right," he said huskily. He drew her closer with her precious bundle in her arms. "My God, we've had a rocky road. I hope things will be a little smoother for us now."

She reached up and kissed him with aching tenderness. "Stand back and see how smooth. I'll love you to death," she whispered huskily.

He actually flushed, his darkening eyes almost a statement of intent.

"Want me to try?" she murmured provocatively, parting her lips to draw his eyes to them.

"Are you serious?" he asked unsteadily. "Come here."

But before he could get further, their son let out a wail and went searching for the rest of his lunch.

Tess laughed as he found it, smiling at the ferocity of her son's furious expression. She looked at Dane, and the love in his eyes made her warm all over.

"It seems that my son has priorities," he mused, fighting down the surge of desire. "But there's always tonight."

"Yes. I love you," she whispered.

"I love you, too, little one. So much!"

She nibbled softly at his lips. "When John starts school, how would you feel about letting me go back to work?"

He lifted his head. "As a skip tracer for Short?" he asked.

"As an operative for *you*," she corrected.

He pursed his lips. "Keeping it in the family, I gather?"

"Until John is old enough to look good in a trench coat," she agreed.

He hugged her close and drew his fingers lovingly over his son's head. He hesitated, but she looked determined. Well, if he taught her, and watched the cases she took, he could keep her safe. It wouldn't hurt to let her feel independent. At the same time, he wouldn't really mind having her underfoot half the time. He smiled at just the prospect. "Okay. But you'll start out as a skip tracer, and no Mike Hammer stuff, got that?"

"Of course!"

She leaned her head on his chest and smiled at their son. But behind her back, where she was sure he couldn't see them, her fingers were crossed. Seconds later, his smile almost a declaration of love, he reached slowly behind her. And uncrossed them.

* * * * *

From the popular author of the bestselling title
DUNCAN'S BRIDE (Intimate Moments #349)
comes the

LINDA HOWARD

COLLECTION

Two exquisite collector's editions that contain four of
Linda Howard's early passionate love stories. To add
these special volumes to your own library, be sure
to look for:

VOLUME ONE: *Midnight Rainbow*
Diamond Bay
(Available in March)

VOLUME TWO: *Heartbreaker*
White Lies
(Available in April)

 *Silhouette Books*®

SLH92

Take 4 bestselling love stories FREE

Plus get a FREE surprise gift!

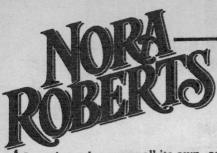